Reflecting Alice

Reflecting Alice
A Textual Commentary on
Through the Looking-Glass

By

Lewis Carroll

ILLUSTRATED BY
JOHN TENNIEL

INTRODUCTION AND ANNOTATIONS BY
SELWYN GOODACRE

evertype
2021

Published by Evertype, 19A Corso Street, Dundee, DD2 1DR, Scotland.
www.evertype.com.

Introduction and annotations © 2021 Selwyn Goodacre.
This edition © 2021 Michael Everson.

First edition December 2021. Reprinted with corrections March 2022.

A catalogue record for this book is available from the British Library.

ISBN-10 1-78201-223-0
ISBN-13 978-1-78201-223-8

Typeset in De Vinne Text, Mona Lisa, ENGRAVERS' ROMAN, and *Liberty* by
Michael Everson.

Illustrations: John Tenniel, 1865.

Cover: Michael Everson.

For Mark Burstein,
who has done such fine work in revising
The Annotated Alice. He has my greatest admiration.

Preface

$\mathcal{I}$ said in the preface to *Elucidating Alice,* that one would have every right to say—"surely we already have an *Annotated Alice*?" And this remains true—and even more so in its latest re-incarnation (*The Annotated Alice, 150th Anniversary de luxe edition,* by Lewis Carroll, edited by Martin Gardner, expanded and updated by Mark Burstein: W W Norton & Company, New York 2015). I continue to be a great admirer of this fine achievement. Martin Gardner's and Mark Burstein's work is unassailable in their explanations of so many elements in the *Alice* books.

But my own approach remains quite different. I wanted to look at the *Alice* books essentially simply as children's books, perhaps even as children's novels, to look at the narrative structure, analyse the way it is put together, and see how Carroll successfully constructed pioneer books for children that were to stand the test of time, remaining totally relevant to the present day. Just as with *Wonderland,* there are many depths and subtleties in *Looking-Glass* that can only be properly evaluated by examining the text line by line. The writing is supremely skilful, and will stand the closest scrutiny—even virtually to every line of the narrative.

Most books would crumble under such line-by-line analysis. It is testimony to the strength, depth, and quality of the *Alice* books that they come through such intense examination and survives triumphantly

Whether I have been successful is for the reader to judge. From my point of view, I can only say that with every re-reading I find fresh nuances and delights.

Selwyn Goodacre
Woodville, South Derbyshire, 2021

Introduction

In a letter to his publisher Macmillan on 24 August 1866, Lewis Carroll wrote "It will probably be some time before I again indulge in paper and print. I have, however, a floating idea of writing a sort of sequel to Alice". John Tenniel initially refused to illustrate a second volume, so in January 1867 Carroll approached Noel Paton, who told him that Tenniel really was "*the* man". Tenniel remained adamant and suggested Richard Doyle. Carroll wrote to him in January 1867 to no avail. In spite of all this, on 6 February 1867 Carroll was able to write to Macmillan "I am hoping before long to complete another book about *Alice*."

Negotiations concerning an illustrator prevented him from making much progress with the book, and it was only with John Tenniel's final agreement, in June 1868, to follow up his illustrations for *Alice's Adventures in Wonderland*, that Carroll finally set about completing *Through the Looking-Glass*. Much has been made of a meeting with Alice Raikes in August 1868 when he asked her in which hand her reflection was holding an orange—She said "The left hand". "How do you explain that?" Carroll replies. "If I were on the *other* side of the glass, wouldn't the orange still be in my right hand?"

Carroll called this "the best answer I have had yet." It is a nice story, but of doubtful significance in the concept of the book, as it was already well advanced by that stage.

Tenniel's rough sketches for some of the illustrations were ready by January 1870. Carroll completed the text by early January 1871. He had problems over the title—initially he tried *The World behind the Looking-Glass, and what Alice found there,* and *Behind the Looking-Glass, and What Alice Saw There.* Another possibility was *Looking-Glass House, and What Alice Saw There.* He eventually settled on *Through the Looking-Glass, and What Alice Found There*, which remains rather clumsy. Why he did not simply call the book *Alice Through the Looking-Glass* is one of life's mysteries.

It is notoriously difficult for any writer to write a sequel to a successful first book. Few have succeeded. In the field of Children's Literature it rarely happens. A. A. Milne managed it with his two books on *Winnie-the-Pooh*, and Lewis Carroll managed it supremely with *Through the Looking-Glass*, many authors like Enid Blyton and Richmal Crompton avoided the problem simply by writing endless sequels of varying quality.

Alice's Adventures in Wonderland was a pioneer work of English Children's Literature, breaking new ground in many ways. From the idea of a child exploring strange lands, to the liberal use of anthropomorphic animals, to a witty understated appraisal of contemporary society, the book set high standards for children's literature to come.

In addition, Lewis Carroll used the highly original idea that a child's book can be a vehicle for humour and can incorporate a highly sophisticated brand of "nonsense". Yet at the same time his book would include insights not only into logic and mathematics, but also into the English Language itself.

To maintain this high level of creativity into a "follow up" volume is nothing short of miraculous. As this is a sequel, Lewis Carroll stays with the same heroine, but she is now slightly older and more worldly wise. He is keen to emphasize that the book is indeed a sequel—he even manages to include Alice's cat Dinah, who, as in *Wonderland*, plays a prominent part in the opening section of the book. The rather episodic nature of the first book is used again in *Looking-Glass* but as this is more of a planned book (*Wonderland* was much more extemporé in origin), Carroll can use a more structured remit. To maintain the continuity with *Wonderland* he again is looking for a basic scenario that incorporates Kings and Queens. Happily he was teaching Chess to Alice Liddell and her sisters, so was able to use this background to happy and fruitful effect.

He then incorporates one of his most famous poetic inventions, the poem *Jabberwocky*, which he had written some years before. In a totally innovative way, this remarkable poem plays with the way words and phrases are structured, and Carroll elaborates on this to such an extent that it becomes an integral part of *Looking-Glass*. He so liked the poem that he originally wanted Tenniel's picture of the Jabberwock for the frontispiece, but decided, after consultation, that it was far too startling an image, and wisely substituted the gentle picture of the bumbling White Knight.

There is an assurance in *Looking-Glass* that is possibly a little lacking in *Wonderland*, Carroll is now more confident, and can organize the whole book using a game of Chess as a basis. His heroine Alice can cope with the various strange characters she meets with greater ease than she managed in *Wonderland*. Alice is treated rather more deferentially in *Looking-Glass* than ever she was in *Wonderland*. Here she can hold her own brilliantly with the Red Queen, she can be motherly towards the White Queen, sisterly towards the Tweedles, argumentative with Humpty Dumpty, and almost parental with the White Knight.

Such is the fertility of Carroll's imagination that he is able to create a whole new cast list of memorable characters, fully up to the originality of the characters in *Wonderland*—and just as with the earlier book, these characters were destined to become memorable well outside the confines of the book itself. In *Wonderland* he tended to personalize English phrases (Mad as a Hatter, Mock Turtle Soup, etc.) for his characters; in *Looking-Glass* he appropriates known Nursery Rhyme characters and makes them all his own. His Humpty Dumpty for example is a total triumph, to the extent that his utterances have become delightfully authoritative, way beyond his humble origins within his nursery rhyme.

The book opens with a possibly over-long discursive passage featuring Alice on her own. In *Wonderland* there was something similar, but at least in that book there was plenty of action (running, falling down wells etc)—here the opening, verging on the overly domestic, is more closely aimed at a female audience, unlike the mixed audience intended for *Wonderland*. It does, however, give our author chance to introduce Alice's thoughts on the problems of just what might be beyond the other side of a mirror.

Lewis Carroll, fully in tune with his heroine, goes along with this, and is happy to make specific points arising out of the concept of going through a looking-glass—so he plays with the ideas of reflection, reversal, positives and negatives ("birthday/unbirthday") and inverted (and indeed, inventive) language, extending this into discussions on believing the impossible (itself something of a reversal) and to the changing meaning of words. Can "tomorrow" ever be "today"? But these points are never allowed to take over the whole book. Alice may well be advised to walk in the opposite direction in order to meet the Red Queen, but elsewhere in the book she can walk quite straightforwardly to meet other characters. In a further memorable episode in her first contact with the Red Queen, Alice has to run fast to stay in order to stay in the same place—but this is a single event, not repeated elsewhere in the book.

The White Queen can demonstrate a very plausible case for cause and effect to be reversed (as when she applies dressings, then bleeds, then screams, and only then pricks herself with the brooch pin)—but at other times things happen in the more usual ordered fashion. The White Knight can discuss what the name of a song is called, or what the name of the song is, or what the song is called, or what the song actually is, and be distressed when Alice does not understand—but this does not seem to be a problem with others reciting poems.

Throughout the book, almost as if he suddenly thinks of it, and inserts it into the text—Carroll has further quirky thoughts about all things to do with reversal, ideas of reflection, thinking backwards, thinking impossible things, the order of days in a week, whether two eyes a nose and a mouth in their customary position are necessary for a face. And he is endlessly intrigued with the meaning of words. The White King:

> "I see nobody on the road," said Alice.
> "I only wish *I* had such eyes," the King remarked in a fretful tone. "To be able to see Nobody!"

And the Frog Gardener:

> "Where's the servant whose business it is to answer the door?" she began angrily
> "To answer the door?" he said. "What's it been asking of?"

Humpty Dumpty on a more conscious level has a wonderful time with *his* use of words—paying them, making them mean whatever he chooses:

> "There's glory for you!"
> "I don't know what you mean by 'glory,'"

Humpty Dumpty smiled contemptuously. "Of course you don't—till I tell you. I meant 'there's a nice knock-down argument for you!'"

But 'glory' doesn't mean 'a nice knock-down argument'." Alice objected.

"When *I* use a word," Humpty Dumpty said in rather a scornful tone, "it means just what I choose it to mean—neither more nor less."

In a nice touch later in the book, Carroll agrees with Humpty Dumpty's meaning of "Glory" when the White Knight defeats the Red Knight by knocking him off his horse, and says to Alice

"It was a glorious victory, wasn't it?"

Isolating them as specific episodes never jars, one reads on barely noticing, so skilfully is it all done. Their very isolation has lead to quotations that have become famous in their own right, ever since:

"It takes all the running *you* can do, to keep in the same place."

"The rule is, jam to-morrow and jam yesterday- but never jam *to-day*."

"When *I* use a word in means just what I choose it to mean—neither more nor less."

In a quite different approach to the English Language, Lewis Carroll, just as he has previously done with *Wonderland*, has huge fun with simple phrases—sometimes returning to the same one. Several characters in *Wonderland* apologize—normally as "I beg your pardon" (the Mouse to the Lory, the Hatter to the

Queen at the trial, and Alice herself four times). None is challenged—it is very different in *Looking-Glass*

> "I beg your pardon?" Alice said with a puzzled air.
> "I'm not offended," said Humpty Dumpty.

> "I beg your pardon?" said Alice.
> "It isn't respectable to beg," said the King.

The link with *Wonderland* is never far away. Apart from Alice herself, and Dinah, other characters reappear, slightly "'adjusted'"—most notably with "Hatta" and "Haigha" but Lewis Carroll never overstates his case. The links are there for the reader to discover, he will not point them out directly.

The links between chapters in *Wonderland* are pretty basic—Alice walks on from one encounter to the next in a fairly ingenuous fashion. In *Looking-Glass* it is all rather more structured. Admittedly, Carroll has less of a problem here as the move from one confrontation to the next has a certain inevitability about it, as she follows the moves of the chess game (which is outlined in detail at the beginning of the book). Even so, there is an extra fluidity in how she encounters each character or set of characters.

She glides from the house into the garden (Chapter II). In Chapter III, in magical fashion she finds herself unexpectedly in the railway carriage—then the talking Gnat magically grows in size and takes over centre stage. It leaves as it "sighs itself away". After the interlude with the fawn, she then "Wonderland-style" in Chapter IV comes upon the Tweedles.

The confrontation with the White Queen (Chapter V) is masterfully initiated—the Monstrous Crow's wings blow in the Queen's shawl, swiftly followed by the Queen herself.

Magical changes of scene abound in *Looking-Glass*—far more so than they ever did in *Wonderland*—Alice suddenly finds herself in the railway carriage; the Queen metamorphoses into the Sheep—who, along with Alice, moves magically from shop to boat and back to shop again. Humpty Dumpty moves from being an egg on a shelf to a very real being sitting on a wall. Chess pieces become life-size, the gnat becomes huge, and flying elephants can sip nectar from flowers. It is so beautifully described, that one accepts it all totally.

The fall of Humpty Dumpty leads in the most natural way into the major scene with the White King, the Lion and Unicorn, and assembled company. The Nursery Rhyme is acted out, leading to the drums drumming "them out of town"—leaving Alice alone—a dramatically solitary quiet moment, swiftly interrupted by the only "chess capture" of the entire book—the defeat of the Red Knight by the White Knight. And so we move to the two-chapter dialogue with the White Knight—again a fitting, and fairly quiet prelude to the climax of the book where Alice at last reaches the Eighth Square and becomes a Queen.

Just as with *Wonderland* the final denouement features several characters we have met earlier in the book. Many readers might find the apocalyptic end rather "over the top"- the White Queen drowns, bottles, plates and a soup ladle become animated and threatening—the Red Queen is violently shaken, and in the last metamorphosis of the book, turns into the black kitten—and Alice wakes.

In a final literary joke, matching the textual intricacies of the Mouse's tail in *Wonderland*, Lewis Carroll has fun with absurdly short chapters just before the end of the book, leading rather charmingly to the close where Alice herself (not her elder sister, as in *Wonderland*) looks back on the adventures, and wonders about the nature of dreams.

Looking-Glass is a brilliant sequel—it is not a re-run of *Wonderland* but rather a most satisfying "further adventure", with new insights and new themes, all totally original. There are, of course, similarities; both books feature Royalty; in both books Alice undertakes a journey, in which she triumphs over all she comes across. She is the same child still, as Lewis Carroll was later to put it—"Loving, first, loving and gentle... then courteous—courteous to all, high or low, grand or grotesque, King or Caterpillar... then trustful, ready to accept the wildest impossibilities with all that utter trust that only dreamers know."

The book has never quite achieved the fame of *Wonderland,* nevertheless it has remained in print since it was first published. As time has gone by, many readers have tended to view the two books as one—sadly many film and stage adaptations get the two hopelessly confused, with the wrong characters appearing at the wrong times, but that I suppose is inevitable, though the purists among us still see the books as quite separate masterpieces. Some years ago the Lewis Carroll Society held a debate on which was the greater book. We came to no firm conclusion, though the level of argument was passionate and vocal.

Acknowledgements

*I*n my book *Elucidating Alice* I discussed how it grew out of various talks I had given to the Lewis Carroll Society, and the Lewis Carroll Society of North America. I am encouraged by their response to that book to undertake this current sequel.

Indeed I continue to be most grateful to the members for their continued support and encouragement

A NOTE ON THE TEXT

As with the text of *Alice's Adventures in Wonderland*, Lewis Carroll made a number of alterations over the years to the text of *Through the Looking-Glass*, though not nearly as many as he had done with *Wonderland*. A number appeared in the People's Edition of 1887,[1] but these were not incorporated in his final revised text of 1897 (the 61st Thousand),[2] so for this edition

1 Goodacre, Selwyn. 1973. "Lewis Carroll's 1887 Corrections to *Alice*", in *The Library*, June 1973.

2 Goodacre, Selwyn. 2008 "Lewis Carroll's Alterations for the 1897 6s. edition of *Through the Looking-Glass*", in *The Carrollian*, Autumn 2008.

we have simply used the 1897 revised text—with certain corrections, and elimination of errors.

Lewis Carroll did make a number of changes to the preliminary matter of the book[3] over the years, and rather curiously omitted the *Dramatis Personae* in the final 1897 revision. We have reinstated it.

As with *Elucidating Alice,* we have added *Christmas Greetings* and *An Easter Greeting,* and *To all child readers of "Alice's Adventures in Wonderland"* (this was written in 1871, as a leaflet to be inserted in copies of the first edition of *Through the Looking-Glass,* and some 1872 editions of *Alice's Adventures in Wonderland*). Only part of the preface to the 61st thousand is used (the rest of the preface relates to details of the printing of the edition in 1897, and details of the price reduction for *The Nursery "Alice"* in 1896).

---

3   Shaberman, Raphael and Selwyn Goodacre. 1978. "Towards the 61st Thousand of *Through the Looking-Glass*", in *Jabberwocky, The Journal of the Lewis Carroll Society,* Spring 1978.

Through the Looking-Glass and What Alice Found There

ON THE CHESS REPERTOIRES

The *Dramatis Personae* presented on page 3 was not included in the final revision of 1897. Was this because Lewis Carroll realised it includes numerous inconsistencies with elements that seem totally arbitrary? For an excellent discussion on this, see *The Annotated Alice*.

As with the *Dramatis Personae*, the chess-problem given on p. 4 also presents several problems. Some are discussed by Lewis Carroll himself (see his *Preface*, p. 5 below), but for a more detailed analysis, again see *The Annotated Alice*.

DRAMATIS PERSONÆ

(As arranged before commencement of game.)

WHITE.   RED.

PIECES	PAWNS	PAWNS	PIECES
Tweedledee	Daisy.	Daisy	Humpty Dumpty
Unicorn	Haigha.	Messenger	Carpenter
Sheep	Oyster.	Oyster	Walrus.
W. Queen	"Lily".[4]	Tiger-lily	R. Queen.
W. King	Fawn.	Rose	R. King.
Aged man	Oyster.	Oyster	Crow.
W. Knight	Hatta.	Frog	R. Knight.
Tweedledum	Daisy.	Daisy	Lion.

---

4   *Lily*—later to be replaced by
Alice herself.

White Pawn (Alice) to play, and win in eleven moves.

RED.

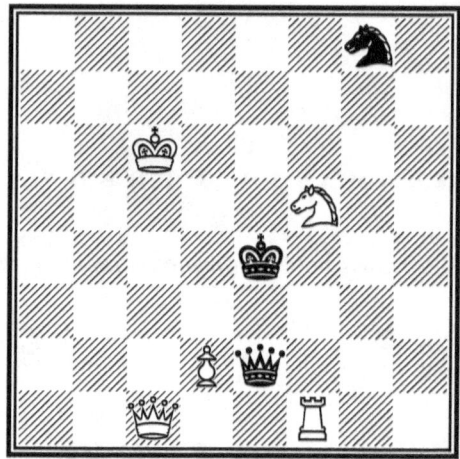

WHITE.

As the chess-problem, given on a previous page, has puzzled some of my readers, it may be well to explain that it is correctly worked out, so far as the *moves* are concerned. The *alternation* of Red and White is perhaps not so strictly observed as it might be, and the "castling" of the three Queens is merely a way of saying that they entered the palace; but the "check" of the White King at move 6, the capture of the Red Knight at move 7, and the final "checkmate" of the Red King, will be found, by any one[5] who will take the trouble to set the pieces and play the moves as directed, to be strictly in accordance with the laws of the game.

The new words, in the poem "Jabberwocky" (see p. 26), have given rise to some differences of opinion as to their pronunciation: so it may be well to give instructions on *that* point also. Pronounce "slithy" as if it were the two words "sly,

---

5   *any one*—as with his use of a two word "some one" Lewis Carroll appears to
    prefer "anyone" to be two words as well—a rather idiosyncratic use, but
    employed consistently throughout both *Alice* books. Similarly he occasionally
    prefers "every thing" to "everything" (see for example in Chapter IV, where
    he changes one instance from one word to two words, to bring it into line with
    the second use, though elsewhere in the book, the single word is used).

the":[6] make the "g" *hard* in "gyre"[7] and "gimble": and pronounce "rath" to rhyme with "bath."[8]

---

6 *"sly, the"*—a curious instruction, as "the" is surely never pronounced with a short "i"? (Michael Everson notes that "the" is pronounced [ði:] before vowels and [ðə] before consonants.)

7 *make the "g" hard in "gyre"*—a curious instruction, as the "g" is soft in "gyroscope" from which the word is derived (see Chapter VI)—or was it a hard "g" in Victorian England? (Michael Everson notes that *gyre* 'to whirl, to gyrate', a word borrowed into late Middle English, is today pronounced both ['dʒʌɪə] and ['gʌɪə]. Compare the graphics format *gif*, pronounced both [dʒɪf] and [gɪf].)

8 *pronounce "rath" to rhyme with "bath"*—Lewis Carroll is playing with us. His suggestion does not help at all. "Bath" can be pronounced [bɑːθ] as in "hearth" (standard English) or [baθ] as in "hath" (northern English).

Contents

Child of the pure unclouded brow[9]
   And dreaming eyes of wonder!
Though time be fleet, and I and thou[10]
   Are half a life asunder,
Thy loving smile will surely hail
The love-gift of a fairy-tale.[11]

I have not seen thy sunny face
   Nor heard thy silver laughter:
No thought of me shall find a place
   In thy young life's hereafter—
Enough that now thou wilt not fail
To listen to my fairy-tale.

A tale begun in other days,
   When summer suns were glowing—[12]
A simple chime, that served to time
   The rhythm of our rowing—
Whose echoes live in memory yet,
Though envious years would say "forget."

---

9   The rhyming structure varies through the poem. Verses 1, 2, 4, 5, 6 have ABABCC, verse 3 has ABCBDD.

10 Curiously, Carroll uses old style "thee" and "thou" etc. throughout the poem. It adds a nostalgic feel, which is a major element of the poem.

11 The motif "fairy-tale" is used at the end of verses 1, 2 and 6, a clear indication that Carroll views the *Alice* books as fairy tales (see my notes in *Elucidating Alice*).

12 *When summer suns were glowing*—the first indication that the story, in contrast to *Alice's Adventures in Wonderland*, is to take place in autumn or winter.

Come, hearken then, ere voice of dread,
    With bitter tidings laden,
Shall summon to unwelcome bed
    A melancholy maiden!
We are but older children, dear,
Who fret to find our bedtime near.[13]

Without, the frost, the blinding snow,[14]
    The storm-wind's moody madness—
Within, the firelight's ruddy glow,
    And childhood's nest of gladness.
The magic words shall hold thee fast:
Thou shalt not heed the raving blast.

And, though the shadow of a sigh
    May tremble through the story,
For "happy summer days"[15] gone by,
    And vanish'd summer glory[16]—
It shall not touch, with breath of bale,
The pleasance of our fairy-tale.

---

13   This verse is so obviously referring to a child's reluctance to go to bed, that it is simply perverse to imply any sexual element, as some writers have done.

14   Another indication that the story, in contrast to *Alice's Adventures in Wonderland*, will take place in autumn or winter.

15   *"happy summer days"*—*The Annotated Alice* reminds us that these words are in inverted commas as they recall the last words of *Wonderland*.

16   *vanish'd summer glory*—the final reference is an indication that the story is likely to take place in autumn or winter.

INTRODUCTION TO CHAPTER I

*T*he opening section is quite lengthy, and is entirely taken up with Alice coping with Dinah's kittens. Once Alice is through the Looking-glass, her playful activity continues with parental type behaviour with the White King, White Queen, and White Knight. Curiously, all behave in a quite different way to how they appear later in the book—in fully adult form, as it were.

The concept of reversal when "through the looking-glass" is introduced gradually—starting with her finding the book with Jabberwocky in reverse type. She manages to exit the house with little difficulty, and only finds problems when she reaches the garden.

L o o k i n g – G l a s s   H o u s e

$\mathcal{O}$ ne thing was certain, that the *white* kitten had had nothing to do with it—it was the black kitten's fault entirely.[17] For the white kitten had been having its face washed by the old cat for the last quarter of an hour (and bearing it pretty well, considering): so you see that it *couldn't* have had any hand in the mischief.

The way Dinah[18] washed her children's faces was this: first she held the poor thing down by its ears with one paw, and then with the other paw she rubbed its face all over, the wrong way, beginning at the nose: and just now, as I said, she was hard at work on the white kitten, which was lying quite still and trying to purr—no doubt feeling that it was all meant for its good.

But the black kitten had been finished with earlier in the afternoon, and so, while Alice was sitting curled up in a

17   *white/black*—although not stated, this early emphasis on white and black foreshadows the white/red chess motif of the whole book.

18   *Dinah*—our author does not "introduce" Dinah—he assumes a knowledge in his readers of her from her role in *Alice's Adventures in Wonderland*.

corner of the great arm-chair, half talking to herself and half asleep,[19] the kitten had been having a grand game of romps with the ball of worsted[20] Alice had been trying to wind up, and had been rolling it up and down till it had all come undone again; and there it was, spread over the hearth-rug, all knots and tangles, with the kitten running after its own tail in the middle.

"Oh, you wicked wicked little thing!" cried Alice, catching up the kitten, and giving it a little kiss to make it understand that it was in disgrace. "Really, Dinah ought to have taught you better manners! You *ought*, Dinah, you know you ought!" she added,[21] looking reproachfully at the old cat, and speaking in as cross a voice as she could manage—and then she scrambled back into the arm-chair, taking the kitten and the worsted with her, and began winding up the ball again. But she didn't get on very fast, as she was talking all the time, sometimes to the kitten, and sometimes to herself. Kitty[22] sat very demurely on her knee, pretending to watch the progress of the winding, and now and then putting out

19   *half asleep*—as with the previous volume, we have an early intimation that Alice may be likely to fall asleep and dream...

20   *worsted*—a slightly old fashioned word—meaning a woolen yarn.

21   A rather delightful portrayal of Alice's ironic and gentle humour.

22   *Kitty*—the first mention of the black kitten's name.

one paw and gently touching the ball, as if it would be glad to help if it might.

"Do you know what to-morrow is, Kitty?" Alice began. "You'd have guessed if you'd been up in the window[23] with me—only Dinah was making you tidy, so you couldn't. I was watching the boys[24] getting in sticks for the bonfire[25]—and it wants plenty of sticks, Kitty! Only it got so cold, and it snowed so,[26] they had to leave off. Never mind, Kitty, we'll go and see the bonfire to-morrow." Here Alice wound two or three turns of the worsted round the kitten's neck, just to see how it would look: this led to a scramble, in which the ball rolled down upon the floor, and yards and yards of it got unwound again.

"Do you know, I was so angry, Kitty," Alice went on, as soon as they were comfortably settled again, "when I saw all the mischief you had been doing, I was very nearly opening the window, and putting you out into the snow! And you'd have deserved it, you little mischievous darling! What have you got to say for yourself? Now don't interrupt me!" she went on, holding up one finger. "I'm going to tell you all your faults. Number one: you squeaked twice while Dinah was washing your face this morning. Now you ca'n't deny it, Kitty: I heard you! What's that you say?" (pretending that the kitten was speaking). "Her paw went into your eye? Well, that's *your* fault, for keeping your eyes open—if you'd shut them tight up, it wouldn't have happened. Now don't make any more excuses, but listen! Number two: you pulled

---

23 *up in the window*—though not stated this really means she is on a ledge by the window—in Victorian homes this was often a place where one could sit comfortably.

24 *watching the boys*—does one assume she is referring to her brothers?

25 *for the bonfire*—our first indication of the date being 4 November (i.e. one day before the celebration of Guy Fawkes with bonfires, fireworks etc.).

26 *it snowed so*—very unusual weather for early November in England.

Snowdrop[27] away by the tail just as I had put down the saucer of milk before her! What, you were thirsty, were you? How do you know she wasn't thirsty too? Now for number three: you unwound every bit of the worsted while I wasn't looking!

"That's three faults, Kitty, and you've not been punished for any of them yet. You know I'm saving up all your punishments for Wednesday week— suppose they had saved up all *my* punishments?" she went on, talking more to herself than the kitten. "What *would* they do at the end of a year? I should be sent to prison, I suppose, when the day came. Or—let me see—suppose each punishment was to be going without a

27   *Snowdrop*—we now know the name of the white kitten, who is designated as female, whilst Kitty remains neuter.

dinner: then, when the miserable day came, I should have to go without fifty dinners at once! Well, I shouldn't mind *that* much! I'd far rather go without them than eat them![28]

"Do you hear the snow against the window-panes, Kitty? How nice and soft it sounds! Just as if some one[29] was kissing the window all over outside. I wonder if the snow *loves* the trees and fields, that it kisses them so gently? And then it covers them up snug, you know, with a white quilt; and perhaps it says 'Go to sleep, darlings, till the summer comes again.' And when they wake up in the summer,[30] Kitty, they dress themselves all in green, and dance about—whenever the wind blows—oh, that's very pretty!" cried Alice, dropping the ball of worsted to clap her hands. "And I do so *wish* it was true! I'm sure the woods look sleepy in the autumn, when the leaves are getting brown.

"Kitty, can you play chess? Now, don't smile, my dear, I'm asking it seriously. Because, when we were playing just now,[31] you watched just as if you understood it: and when I said 'Check!' you purred! Well, it *was* a nice check, Kitty, and really I might have won, if it hadn't been for that nasty Knight, that came wriggling down among my pieces. Kitty,

---

28 *far rather go without them than eat them*—a rather sad comment—reflecting Alice's feelings about Victorian Nursery dinners.

29 *some one*—as with his use of "any one" curiously Lewis Carroll tends to use the two words, rather than combine them as the more conventional "someone". In *Alice's Adventures in Wonderland*, the words are only used once. In *Through the Looking-Glass*, there are three instances.

30 *when they wake up in the summer*—a rather romantic view, implying that the snow remains in situ for the entire winter.

31 *we were playing just now*—presumably with one of her siblings? It is interesting that a sister is mentioned here—the context here, as with the game of kings and queens later in the paragraph, suggests that this is not the elder sister who featured in the previous volume, who would appear to have been an adult—though this elder sister is mentioned several times later in the book.

dear, let's pretend——" and here I wish I could tell you half the things Alice used to say, beginning with her favourite phrase "Let's pretend." She had had quite a long argument with her sister only the day before—all because Alice had begun with "Let's pretend we're kings and queens;" and her sister, who liked being very exact, had argued that they couldn't, because there were only two of them, and Alice had been reduced at last to say "Well, *you* can be one of them, and *I'll* be all the rest." And once she had really frightened her old nurse by shouting suddenly in her ear "Nurse! Do let's pretend that I'm a hungry hyæna, and you're a bone!"

But this is taking us away from Alice's speech to the kitten. "Let's pretend that you're the Red Queen, Kitty![32] Do you know, I think if you sat up and folded your arms, you'd look exactly like her. Now do try, there's a dear!" And Alice got the Red Queen off the table, and set it up before the kitten as a model for it to imitate: however, the thing didn't succeed, principally, Alice said, because the kitten wouldn't fold its arms properly. So, to punish it, she held it up to the Looking-glass,[33] that it might see how sulky it was, "—and if you're not good directly," she added, "I'll put you through into Looking-glass House. How would you like *that?*

"Now, if you'll only attend, Kitty, and not talk so much, I'll tell you all my ideas about Looking-glass House. First, there's the room you can see through the glass—that's just the same as our drawing-room, only the things go the other way. I can see all of it when I get up upon a chair—all but

32 Although Kitty remains neuter, we can only assume she is in fact female, as she is encouraged to imitate the Red Queen, rather than the Red King. The black kitten being encouraged to imitate the Red Queen is the first indication that in the context of the present discussion, 'red' = 'black'— in chess terms at least.

33 *held it up to the Looking-glass*—the first time the looking-glass is mentioned—and given an upper case letter—possibly in view of its importance in the action to come? The upper case continues to be used.

the bit just behind the fire-place. Oh! I do wish I could see *that* bit! I want so much to know whether they've[34] a fire in the winter: you never *can* tell, you know, unless our fire smokes, and then smoke comes up in that room too—but that may be only pretence, just to make it look as if they had a fire. Well then, the books are something like our books, only the words go the wrong way: I know *that*, because I've held up one of our books to the glass, and then they hold up one in the other room.

"How would you like to live in Looking-glass House, Kitty? I wonder if they'd give you milk in there? Perhaps Looking-glass milk isn't good to drink—but oh, Kitty! Now we come to the passage. You can just see a little *peep* of the passage in Looking-glass House, if you leave the door of our drawing-room wide open: and it's very like our passage as far as you can see, only you know it may be quite different on beyond. Oh, Kitty, how nice it would be if we could only get through into Looking-glass House! I'm sure it's got, oh! Such beautiful things in it! Let's pretend there's a way of getting through into it, somehow, Kitty. Let's pretend the glass has got all soft like gauze, so that we can get through. Why, it's turning into a sort of mist now, I declare! It'll be easy enough to get through——" she was up on the chimney-piece[35] while she said this, though she hardly knew how she had got there.

34 This is all rather whimsical. Alice appears to be suggesting a whole race of people populating the "other side" of the looking-glass—with her reference to "they". She makes no comment on the reflection of herself, so we are spared any anguished discussion about doppelgangers.

35 It would appear that she has left Kitty on the chair, as she is not mentioned again until the end of the book. Alice "hardly knew how she got there"— which suggests she is already experiencing the way she leaves the house in Chapter II, i.e. she is already asleep and dreaming. Alice's forays onto mantelpieces over a lit fire would not pass health and safety regulations these days. Our author's use of the word "chimney-piece" is strange, "mantel-piece" would be rather more appropriate, one would have thought.

And certainly the glass *was* beginning to melt away, just like a bright silvery mist.

In another moment Alice was through the glass, and had jumped lightly down into the Looking-glass room. The very first thing she did was to look whether there was a fire in the fireplace, and she was quite pleased to finds that there was a real one, blazing away as brightly as the one she had left behind. "So I shall be as warm here as I was in the old room," thought Alice: "warmer, in fact, because there'll be no one here to scold me away from the fire.[36] Oh, what fun it'll be, when they see me through the glass in here, and ca'n't get at me!"

36 *scold me away from the fire*—fireguards would appear be to items of the future.

Then she began looking about, and noticed that what could be seen from the old room was quite common and uninteresting, but that all the rest was as different as possible. For instance, the pictures on the wall next the fire seemed to be all alive, and the very clock on the chimney-piece (you know you can only see[37] the back of it in the Looking-glass) had got the face of a little old man, and grinned at her.

"They don't keep this room so tidy as the other," Alice thought to herself, as she noticed several of the chessmen

37   *you know you can only see*—the first time that our author addresses the reader directly. There are four more instances in the book (on thinking in chorus, on scented rushes, on paying words, and the final words of the book).

down in the hearth among the cinders; but in another moment, with a little "Oh!" of surprise, she was down on her hands and knees watching them. The chessmen were walking about, two and two!

"Here are the Red King and the Red Queen," Alice said (in a whisper, for fear of frightening them), "and there are the White King and the White Queen sitting on the edge of the shovel—and here are two Castles walking arm in arm—I don't think they can hear me," she went on, as she put her head closer down, "and I'm nearly sure they ca'n't see me. I feel somehow as if I was getting invisible——"[38]

Here something began squeaking on the table behind Alice, and made her turn her head just in time to see one of the White Pawns roll over and begin kicking: she watched it with great curiosity to see what would happen next.

"It is the voice of my child!" the White Queen cried out, as she rushed past the King, so violently that she knocked him over among the cinders. "My precious Lily! My imperial kitten!"[39] and she began scrambling wildly up the side of the fender.

"Imperial fiddlestick!" said the King, rubbing his nose, which had been hurt by the fall. He had every right to be a *little* annoyed with the Queen, for he was covered with ashes from head to foot.

Alice was very anxious to be of use, and, as the poor little Lily was nearly screaming herself into a fit, she hastily picked up the Queen and set her on the table by the side of her noisy little daughter.[40]

38 *getting invisible*—in fact it would appear that the process is already complete, rather than being in progress.

39 *imperial kitten*—is this a gentle reminder to the reader of the link with Alice's kittens from earlier?

40 *little daughter*—the implication here is that all eight white pawns are her offspring. How Lily has got onto the table in the first place has not been vouchsafed to us.

The Queen gasped, and sat down: the rapid journey through the air had quite taken away her breath, and for a minute or two she could do nothing but hug the little Lily in silence. As soon as she had recovered her breath a little, she called out to the White King, who was sitting sulkily among the ashes, "Mind the volcano!"

"What volcano?" said the King, looking up anxiously into the fire, as if he thought that was the most likely place to find one.[41]

"Blew—me—up," panted the Queen, who was still a little out of breath. "Mind you come up—the regular way—don't get blown up!"

Alice watched the White King as he slowly struggled from bar to bar, till at last she said "Why, you'll be hours and hours[42] getting to the table, at that rate. I'd far better help

41 A very reasonable thought!

42 *hours and hours*—if that is so, one wonders how Lily got there in the first place.

you, hadn't I?" But the King took no notice of the question: it was quite clear that he could neither hear her nor see her.

So Alice picked him up very gently, and lifted him across more slowly than she had lifted the Queen, that she mightn't take his breath away; but, before she put him on the table, she thought she might as well dust him a little, he was so covered with ashes.

She said afterwards that she had never seen in all her life such a face as the King made, when he found himself held in the air by an invisible hand, and being dusted: he was far too much astonished to cry out, but his eyes and his mouth went on getting larger and larger, and rounder and rounder, till her hand shook so with laughing that he nearly let him drop upon the floor.

"Oh! *Please* don't make such faces, my dear!" she cried out, quite forgetting that the King couldn't hear her. "You make me laugh so that I can hardly hold you! And don't keep your mouth so wide open! All the ashes will get into it—there, now I think you're tidy enough!" she added, as she smoothed his hair, and set him upon the table near the Queen.

The King immediately fell flat on his back, and lay perfectly still; and Alice was a little alarmed at what she had done, and went round the room to see if she could find any water to throw over him. However, she could find nothing but a bottle of ink, and when she got back with it[43] she found he had recovered, and he and the Queen were talking together in a frightened whisper—so low, that Alice could hardly hear what they said.

The King was saying "I assure you, my dear, I turned cold to the very ends of my whiskers!"

To which the Queen replied "You haven't got any whiskers."

"The horror of that moment," the King went on, "I shall never, *never* forget!"

"You will, though," the Queen said, "if you don't make a memorandum of it."

Alice looked on with great interest as the King took an enormous memorandum-book out of his pocket, and began writing. A sudden thought struck her, and she took hold of the end of the pencil, which came some way over his shoulder, and began writing for him.

The poor King looked puzzled and unhappy, and struggled with the pencil for some time without saying anything; but Alice was too strong for him, and at last he panted out "My dear! I really *must* get a thinner pencil. I ca'n't manage this one a bit: it writes all manner of things that I don't intend——"

"What manner of things?" said the Queen, looking over the book (in which Alice had put '*The White Knight is sliding down the poker. He balances very badly*'). "That's not a memorandum of *your* feelings!"[44]

---

43 *got back with it*—suggests that Alice was indeed thinking of throwing ink over the King—not the best idea, one would have thought.

44 Alice has certainly been enjoying her time as a type of "deus ex machina"—

2 4

There was a book lying near Alice on the table, and while she sat watching the White King (for she was still a little anxious about him, and had the ink all ready to throw[45] over him, in case he fainted again), she turned over the leaves, to find some part that she could read, "—for it's all in some language I don't know," she said to herself.

It was like this.

Jabberwocky

'Twas brillig, and the slithy toves
Did gyre and gimble in the wabe:
All mimsy were the borogoves,
And the mome raths outgrabe

She puzzled over this for some time, but at last a bright thought struck her. "Why, it's a Looking-glass book, of course! And, if I hold it up to a glass, the words will all go the right way again."

This was the poem that Alice read.

---

indeed acting somewhat mischievously.

45   *ink all ready to throw*—Alice still has this idea in mind—oblivious to the problems of damage to the King's clothes and features that would result.

Jabberwocky[46]

'*Twas brillig, and the slithy toves*
    Did gyre and gimble in the wabe:
All mimsy were the borogoves,
    And the mome raths outgrabe.

"*Beware the Jabberwock, my son!*
    The jaws that bite, the claws that catch!
Beware the Jubjub bird, and shun
    The frumious Bandersnatch!"

He took his vorpal sword in hand:
    Long time the manxome foe he sought—
So rested he by the Tumtum tree,
    And stood awhile in thought.

And as in uffish thought he stood,
    The Jabberwock, with eyes of flame,
Came whiffling through the tulgey wood,
    And burbled as it came!

One, two! One, two! And through and through
    The vorpal blade went snicker-snack!
He left it dead, and with its head
    He went galumphing back.

"*And, hast thou slain the Jabberwock?*
    Come to my arms, my beamish boy!
O frabjous day! Callooh! Callay!"
    He chortled in his joy.

---

46   For Humpty Dumpty's interpretation of some of the "hard words" in the
poem, and for thoughts on the other ones—see Chapter VI.

'Twas brillig, and the slithy toves
    Did gyre and gimble in the wabe:
All mimsy were the borogoves,
    And the mome raths outgrabe.

"It seems very pretty," she said when she had finished it, "but it's *rather* hard to understand!" (You see she didn't like to confess, even to herself, that she couldn't make it out at all.) "Somehow it seems to fill my head with ideas—only I don't exactly know what they are! However, *somebody* killed *something:* that's clear, at any rate——"[47]

"But oh!" thought Alice, suddenly jumping up, "if I don't make haste, I shall have to go back through the Looking-glass, before I've seen what the rest of the house is like! Let's have a look at the garden first!" She was out of the room in a moment, and ran down stairs—or, at least, it wasn't exactly running, but a new invention for getting down stairs quickly and easily, as Alice said to herself. She just kept the tips of her fingers on the hand-rail, and floated gently down[48] without even touching the stairs with her feet: then she floated on through the hall, and would have gone straight out at the door in the same way, if she hadn't caught hold of the door-post. She was getting a little giddy with so much floating in the air, and was rather glad to find herself walking again in the natural way.

---

47   All thoughts of the King and Queen and the other characters have gone from her mind.

48   *floated gently down*—this description would seem to recall dream like activity in the author's own experience (and also evident in the current writer's experience of dreams). We have had a preview when she found herself on the chimney piece prior to going through the Looking-glass. At this stage forward progress seems to be straightforward, in contrast to the problems to come, when she is in the garden.

INTRODUCTION TO CHAPTER II

*T*he first part of the chapter deals with Alice's problems in reaching the top of the hill at the end of the garden. Our author tends to isolate single problems created by the reversal from going "through the looking-glass", rather than letting them interfere with the general action of the book. Alice may have problems here in reaching the hill, but later in the story, she appears to have no difficulty at all regarding forward progress. The chapter has several elements—the problems of forward progress, a conversation with the live flowers, and then the crucial and vital meeting with the Red Queen. It is complex and full of detail, with the promise of much more to come.

CHAPTER II

The Garden of Live Flowers

"I should see the garden far better," said Alice to herself, "if I could get to the top of that hill: and here's a path that leads straight up to it—at least, no, it doesn't do *that*——" (after going a few yards along the path, and turning several sharp corners), "but I suppose it will at last. But how curiously it twists! It's more like a corkscrew than a path! Well, *this* turn goes to the hill, I suppose—no, it doesn't! This goes straight back to the house! Well then, I'll try it the other way."

And so she did: wandering up and down, and trying turn after turn, but always coming back to the house, do what she would. Indeed, once, when she turned a corner rather more quickly than usual, she ran against it before she could stop herself.

"It's no use talking about it," Alice said, looking up at the house and pretending it was arguing with her. "I'm *not* going in again yet. I know I should have to get through the

Looking-glass again—back into the old room—and there'd be an end of all my adventures!"[49]

So, resolutely turning her back upon the house, she set out once more down the path, determined to keep straight on till she got to the hill. For a few minutes all went on well, and she was just saying "I really *shall* do it this time——" when the path gave a sudden twist and shook itself (as she described it afterwards), and the next moment she found herself actually walking in at the door.

"Oh, it's too bad!" she cried. "I never saw such a house for getting in the way! Never!"

However, there was the hill full in sight, so there was nothing to be done but start again. This time she came upon a large flower-bed, with a border of daisies, and a willow-tree growing in the middle.

"O Tiger-lily!" said Alice, addressing herself to one that was waving gracefully about in the wind, "I *wish* you could talk!"

"We *can* talk," said the Tiger-lily, "when there's anybody worth talking to."

Alice was so astonished that she couldn't speak for a minute: it quite seemed to take her breath away.[50] At length, as the Tiger-lily only went on waving about, she spoke again, in a timid voice—almost in a whisper. "And can *all* the flowers talk?"[51]

"As well as *you* can," said the Tiger-lily. "And a great deal louder."

---

49 *my adventures*—a conscious reference to her earlier 'adventures' in Wonderland?

50 Alice's astonishment at the flowers' ability to talk is so great, that she totally forgets, for the time being, that the reason she wants to talk to them is to ask about how she can get to the hill.

51 *And can all the flowers talk?*—the Tiger-lily and the Rose (below) appear to be solitary flowers, rather than one of several, which in a garden is a little odd.

"It isn't manners for us to begin, you know," said the Rose, "and I really was wondering when you'd speak! Said I to myself 'Her face[52] has got *some* sense in it, though it's not a clever one!' Still, you're the right colour,[53] and that goes a long way."

"I don't care about the colour," the Tiger-lily remarked. "If only her petals curled up a little more, she'd be all right."

Alice didn't like being criticized, so she began asking questions. "Aren't you sometimes frightened at being planted out here, with nobody to take care of you?"

"There's the tree in the middle," said the Rose. "What else is it good for?"

"But what could it do, if any danger came?" Alice asked.

"It could bark," said the Rose.

"It says 'Bough-wough!'" cried a Daisy. "That's why its branches are called boughs!"[54]

"Didn't you know *that?*" cried another Daisy. And here they all began shouting together, till the air seemed quite full of little shrill voices. "Silence, every one of you!" cried the Tiger-lily, waving itself passionately from side to side, and trembling with excitement. "They know I ca'n't get at them!" it panted, bending its quivering head towards Alice, "or they wouldn't dare to do it!"

"Never mind!" Alice said in a soothing tone, and, stooping down to the daisies, who were just beginning again, she whispered "If you don't hold your tongues,[55] I'll pick you!"

---

52   *Her face*—the Rose is assuming Alice is a flower, but even so still describes her as female.

53   *the right colour*—one wonders which colour the Rose is referring to, and why it should be "right".

54   Typical word play by our author—he is using two meanings of the word "bark" (though only one is actually stated), the second plays with two quite different words which are pronounced in the same way.

55   *hold your tongues*—though, of course, daisies do not have tongues. Just how they manage to speak is not vouchsafed to us.

There was silence in a moment, and several of the pink daisies turned white.[56]

"That's right!" said the Tiger-lily. "The daisies are worst of all. When one speaks, they all begin together, and it's enough to make one wither to hear the way they go on!"

"How is it you can all talk so nicely?" Alice said, hoping to get it into a better temper by a compliment. "I've been in many gardens before, but none of the flowers could talk."

"Put your hand down, and feel the ground," said the Tiger-lily. "Then you'll know why."

56   *turned white*—one wonders how this could possibly happen; for a possible solution see *The Annotated Alice*.

Alice did so. "It's very hard," she said; "but I don't see what that has to do with it."

"In most gardens," the Tiger-lily said, "they make the beds too soft—so that the flowers are always asleep."

This sounded a very good reason,[57] and Alice was quite pleased to know it. "I never thought of that before!" she said.

"It's *my* opinion that you never think at *all*," the Rose said, in a rather severe tone.

"I never saw anybody that looked stupider," a Violet said, so suddenly, that Alice quite jumped; for it hadn't spoken before.

"Hold *your* tongue!"[58] cried the Tiger-lily. "As if *you* ever saw anybody! You keep your head under the leaves, and snore away there, till you know no more what's going on in the world, than if you were a bud!"

"Are there any more people in the garden besides me?" Alice said, not choosing to notice the Rose's last remark.

"There's one other flower[59] in the garden that can move about like you," said the Rose. "I wonder how you do it——" ("You're always wondering," said the Tiger-lily), "but she's more bushy[60] than you are."

"Is she like me?" Alice asked eagerly, for the thought crossed her mind "There's another little girl in the garden, somewhere!"

"Well, she has the same awkward shape as you," the Rose said: "but she's redder—and her petals are shorter, I think."

"They're done up close, like a dahlia," said the Tiger-Lily: "not tumbled about, like yours."

---

57 *a very good reason*—one could argue the point, but this *is* a book for children, so we will let it pass.

58 *Hold* YOUR *tongue*—for once the Tiger-lily is defending Alice.

59 *There's one other flower*—an odd remark; one would have thought the flowers had met gardeners etc. frequently.

60 *she's more bushy*—in spite of the flowers' assertion that the other "flower" is indeed a flower: as with Alice they describe the "flower" as female.

"But that's not *your* fault," the Rose added kindly. "You're beginning to fade, you know—and then one ca'n't help one's petals getting a little untidy."

Alice didn't like this idea at all: so, to change the subject, she asked "Does she ever come out here?"

"I daresay you'll see her soon," said the Rose.[61] "She's one of the kind that has nine spikes, you know."

"Where does she wear them?" Alice asked with some curiosity.

"Why, all round her head, of course," the Rose replied. "I was wondering *you* hadn't got some too.[62] I thought it was the regular rule."[63]

"She's coming!" cried the Larkspur.[64] "I hear her footstep, thump, thump, along the gravel-walk!"

Alice looked round eagerly and found that it was the Red Queen. "She's grown a good deal!" was her first remark. She had indeed: when Alice first found her in the ashes, she had been only three inches high—and here she was, half a head taller than Alice herself!

"It's the fresh air that does it," said the Rose: "wonderfully fine air it is, out here."[65]

"I think I'll go and meet her," said Alice, for, though the flowers were interesting enough, she felt that it would be far grander to have a talk with a real Queen.

---

61 The Rose had taken over the role, from the Tiger-lily, of chief conversationalist with Alice.

62 *I was wondering* YOU *hadn't got some too*—a prophetic thought—anticipating the crowning of Alice later in the book.

63 *thought it was the regular rule*—again suggesting that the flowers' knowledge of folks in the garden is rather limited.

64 *Larkspur*—her first appearance, and, as Martin Gardner has pointed out, a conscious reference to *Maud*, the poem by Alfred Lord Tennyson.

65 It would appear that Alice and the Rose are talking at cross purposes here. Alice is referring to the huge change in the Queen's size, the Rose, one would assume, is simply talking about normal growth in the fresh air.

"You ca'n't possibly do that," said the Rose: "*I* should advise you to walk the other way."[66]

This sounded nonsense to Alice, so she said nothing, but set off at once towards the Red Queen. To her surprise she lost sight of her in a moment, and found herself walking in at the front-door again.

A little provoked, she drew back, and, after looking everywhere for the Queen (whom she spied out at last, a long way off), she thought she would try the plan, this time, of walking in the opposite direction.

It succeeded beautifully. She had not been walking a minute before she found herself face to face with the Red Queen, and full in sight of the hill she had been so long aiming at.

"Where do you come from?" said the Red Queen. "And where are you going? Look up, speak nicely, and don't twiddle your fingers all the time."[67]

Alice attended to all these directions, and explained, as well as she could, that she had lost her way.

"I don't know what you mean by *your* way," said the Queen: "all the ways about here belong to *me*—but why did you come here at all?" she added in a kinder tone. "Curtsey while you're thinking what to say. It saves time."[68]

Alice wondered a little at this, but she was too much in awe of the Queen to disbelieve it. "I'll try it when I go home," she thought to herself, "the next time I'm a little late for dinner."[69]

---

66   *walk the other way*—although a flower, the Rose now seems to have full knowledge of the walking abilities of Alice and the Queen. The Rose's solution is in fact the reply that Alice was seeking when she first discovered that the flowers could talk—see above.

67   The Red Queen is immediately into "governess-mode".

68   The Queen is implying that it is rude to talk and curtsey at the same time.

69   A slightly odd thought. Why should curtseying help the problem of being late for dinner?

"It's time for you to answer now," the Queen said, looking at her watch: "open your mouth a *little* wider when you speak, and always say 'your Majesty.'"

"I only wanted to see what the garden was like, your Majesty——"

"That's right," said the Queen, patting her on the head, which Alice didn't like at all: "though, when you say 'garden'—*I've* seen gardens, compared with which this would be a wilderness."[70]

70 Again a slightly odd remark—the Queen appears to be suggesting that her own garden is a wilderness in comparison to others she has seen, thus denigrating her own garden.

Alice didn't dare to argue the point, but went on: "—and I thought I'd try and find my way to the top of that hill——"[71]

"When you say 'hill,'" the Queen interrupted, "*I* could show you hills, in comparison with which you'd call that a valley."

"No, I shouldn't," said Alice, surprised into contradicting her at last: "a hill *ca'n't* be a valley, you know. That would be nonsense——"[72]

The Red Queen shook her head. "You may call it 'nonsense' if you like," she said, "but *I've* heard nonsense, compared with which that would be as sensible as dictionary!"

Alice curtseyed again, as she was afraid from the Queen's tone that she was a *little* offended: and they walked on in silence till they got to the top of the little hill.[73]

For some minutes Alice stood without speaking, looking in all directions over the county—and a most curious country it was. There were a number of tiny little brooks[74] running straight across it from side to side, and the ground between was divided up into squares by a number of little green hedges that reached from brook to brook.

"I declare it's marked out just like a large chess-board!" Alice said at last. "There ought to be some men moving about somewhere—and so there are!"[75] she added in a tone of

---

71   Alice again talks about "my way"—but the Queen does not pick up on it this time.

72   Alice is accepting the thought of a garden and wilderness being possible— as they are, just, comparable, whereas hill and valley are opposites.

73   Here, their progress walking to the top of the hill has occurred with none of the problems that occurred when Alice tried to get there earlier. Another indication of our author making only occasional isolated instances of possible problems engendered by looking-glass reversal etc.

74   *There were a number of tiny little brooks*—grammatically speaking, as "number" is a singular noun, it should read *There was a number of little brooks*.

75   It would seem that the game is already being played—so quite how Alice could possibly fit in at this stage is not vouchsafed. Or are "the men moving

delight, and her heart began to beat quick with excitement as she went on. "It's a great huge game of chess that's being played—all over the world—if this *is* the world at all, you know. Oh, what fun it is! How I *wish* I was one of them! I wouldn't mind being a Pawn, if only I might join—though of course I should *like* to be a Queen, best."

She glanced rather shyly at the real Queen as she said this, but her companion only smiled pleasantly, and said "That's easily managed. You can be the White Queen's Pawn, if you like, as Lily's too young to play;[76] and you're in the Second Square to begin with: when you get to the Eighth Square you'll be a Queen——" just at this moment, somehow or other, they began to run.

Alice never could quite make out, in thinking it over afterwards, how it was that they began: all she remembers is,[77] that they were running hand in hand, and the Queen went

about" simply making preparations for the game?

76   We have of course met Lily before—on the table in Looking-Glass house. The Red Queen appears to have the authority to make decisions about replacing Lily with Alice—even though this involves the opposing team.

77   *all she remembers*—the present tense is unusual, possibly an authorial error?

so fast that it was all she could do to keep up with her: and still the Queen kept crying "Faster! Faster!", but Alice felt she *could not* go faster, though she had no breath left to say so.

The most curious part of the thing was, that the trees and the other things round them never changed their places at all: however fast they went, they never seemed to pass anything. "I wonder if all the things move along with us?" thought poor puzzled Alice. And the Queen seemed to guess her thoughts, for she cried "Faster! Don't try to talk!"

Not that Alice had any idea of doing *that*. She felt as if she would never be able to talk again, she was getting so much out of breath: and still the Queen cried "Faster! Faster!", and dragged her along. "Are we nearly there?"[78] Alice managed to pant out at last.

"Nearly there!" the Queen repeated. "Why, we passed it ten minutes ago![79] Faster!" And they ran on for a time in silence,

78   *Are we nearly there?*—it is interesting that Alice does not query the running at this moment, she assumes there is a destination intended, even though she has no idea where or what it might be.

79   *passed it ten minutes ago*—if so, why did they not stop at that point? We are not told what "it" might be. And evidently they have been running for over ten minutes at this stage—a considerable length of time one would

with the wind whistling in Alice's ears and almost blowing her hair off her head, she fancied.

"Now! Now!" cried the Queen. "Faster! Faster!"[80] And they went so fast that at last they seemed to skim through the air, hardly touching the ground with their feet, till suddenly, just as Alice was getting quite exhausted, they stopped, and she found herself sitting on the ground, breathless and giddy.

The Queen propped her up against a tree, and said kindly "You may rest a little, now."

Alice looked round her in great surprise. "Why, I believe we've been under this tree the whole time! Everything's just as it was!"

"Of course it is," said the Queen. "What would you have it?"

"Well, in *our* country," said Alice, still panting a little, "you'd generally get to somewhere else[81]—if you ran very fast for a long time as we've been doing."

"A slow sort of country!" said the Queen. "Now, *here*, you see, it takes all the running *you* can do, to keep in the same place. If you want to get somewhere else, you must run at least twice as fast as that!"[82]

"I'd rather not try, please!" said Alice. "I'm quite content to stay here—only I *am* so hot and thirsty!"

"I know what *you'd* like!" the Queen said good-naturedly, taking a little box out of her pocket. "Have a biscuit?"

Alice thought it would not be civil to say "No," though it wasn't at all what she wanted. So she took it, and ate it as

have thought.

80 The Queen's authority is certainly stamped on this exercise—she urges Alice to go faster no less than five times.

81 *generally get to somewhere else*—for the sake of politeness to the Queen, Alice is being ironic.

82 Logically, with this "rule" one would have thought, one could simply not run at all—and you would be somewhere else?

well as she could: and it was *very* dry:[83] and she thought she had never been so nearly choked in all her life.

"While you're refreshing yourself," said the Queen. "I'll just take the measurements." And she took a ribbon out of her pocket, marked in inches,[84] and began measuring the ground, and sticking little pegs in here and there.

"At the end of two yards," she said, putting in a peg to mark the distance, "I shall give you your directions—have another biscuit?"

"No, thank you," said Alice: "one's *quite* enough!"

"Thirst quenched, I hope?"[85] said the Queen.

Alice did not know what to say to this, but luckily the Queen did not wait for an answer, but went on. "At the end of *three* yards I shall repeat them—for fear of your forgetting them. At the end of *four*, I shall say good-bye. And at the end of *five* I shall go!"

She had got all the pegs put in by this time, and Alice looked on with great interest as she returned to the tree, and then began slowly walking down the row.

At the two-yard peg she faced round, and said "A pawn goes two squares in its first move, you know.[86] So you'll go *very* quickly through the Third Square—by railway, I should think—and you'll find yourself in the Fourth Square in no time. Well, *that* square belongs to Tweedledum and Tweedledee—the Fifth is mostly water—the Sixth belongs to Humpty Dumpty—but you make no remark?"

---

83   *very dry*—although not stated here, one wonders if this is intended as another example of reversal?

84   *ribbon marked in inches*—what we would now call a tape measure.

85   *Thirst quenched*—this would certainly suggest that the Queen believes the concept of reversal.

86   *A pawn goes two squares in its first move*—as we all know this is not quite true—certainly it *can* move two squares for its first move, but this is only an option.

"I—I didn't know I had to make one—just then," Alice faltered out.

"You *should* have said," the Queen went on in a tone of grave reproof, "'It's extremely kind of you to tell me all this'—however, we'll suppose it said—the Seventh Square is all forest—however, one of the Knights will show you the way—and in the Eighth Square, we shall be Queens together, and it's all feasting and fun!"[87] Alice got up and curtseyed, and sat down again.

At the next peg the Queen turned again, and this time she said "Speak in French when you ca'n't think of the English for a thing—turn out your toes as you walk—and remember who you are!"[88] She did no wait for Alice to curtsey, this time, but walked on quickly to the next peg, where she turned for a moment to say "Good-bye," and then hurried on to the last.

How it happened, Alice never knew, but exactly as she came to the last peg, she was gone. Whether she vanished into the air, or whether she ran quickly into the wood ("and she *can* run very fast!" thought Alice), there was no way of guessing, but she was gone, and Alice began to remember that she was a Pawn, and that it would soon by time for her to move.

---

87   The account of Alice's expected progress is an accurate list of what indeed happens in the rest of the book. It would appear that the structure of the game is already decided, in that Alice's progress is anticipated to be virtually unhindered throughout the game.

88   In her initial instructions, the Queen said she would repeat the directions at the end of three yards, but she does not—she gives further instructions instead. But for the fourth and fifth yards she *does* do exactly as she had said she would.

INTRODUCTION TO CHAPTER III

The chapter opens with Alice in conversation with several characters, but moves to more intimate conversations with two characters only—namely the Gnat, and then the Fawn. Both are mostly sympathetic towards Alice, making a pleasant contrast to the earlier confrontation with the Red Queen.

CHAPTER III

Looking-Glass Insects

O f course the first thing to do was to make a grand survey of the country she was going to travel through. "It's something very like learning geography," thought Alice, as she stood on tiptoe in hopes of being able to see a little further. "Principal rivers[89]—there *are* none. Principal mountains—I'm on the only one, but I don't think it's got any name. Principal towns—why, what *are* those creatures, making honey[90] down there? They ca'n't be bees—nobody ever saw bees a mile off, you know——" and for some time she stood silent, watching one of them that was bustling about among the flowers, poking its proboscis into them, "just as if it was a regular bee," thought Alice.

---

89   *Principal rivers*—Alice does not consider that the several little brooks mentioned in the previous chapter qualify as rivers.

90   *making honey*—whether the collection of nectar from flowers is the same as "making honey" is rather telescoping the process.

However, this was anything but a regular bee: in fact, it was an elephant[91]—as Alice soon found out, though the idea quite took her breath away at first. "And what enormous flowers they must be!" was her next idea. "Something like cottages with the roofs taken off, and stalks put to them—and what quantities of honey they must make! I think I'll go down and—no, I wo'n't go *just* yet," she went on, checking herself just as she was beginning to run down the hill, and trying to find some excuse for turning shy so suddenly. "It'll never do to go down among them without a good long branch to brush them away—and what fun it'll be when they ask me how I liked my walk. I shall say 'Oh, I liked it well enough——' (here came the favourite little toss of the head), 'only it *was* so dusty and hot, and the elephants *did* tease so!'

"I think I'll go down the other way," she said after a pause; "and perhaps I may visit the elephants later on.[92] Besides, I *do* so want to get into the Third Square!"

So, with this excuse, she ran down the hill, and jumped over the first of the six little brooks.

"Tickets, please!" said the Guard, putting his head in at the window.[94] In a moment everybody was holding out a

91   *it was an elephant*—if so, one imagines it must have wings, but Alice does not mention them.

92   Sadly this is the last we hear of the elephants.

93   Though not stated, the rows of asterisks denote each of Alice's moves through the chess game, this being the first. The background of the chess game itself, and the various moves involved is fully detailed in *The Annotated Alice*, so I will not be duplicating that in this book.

94   We are not told that Alice is now in a railway carriage, but it rapidly

ticket: they were about the same size as the people, and quite seemed to fill the carriage.

"Now then! Show your ticket, child!" the Guard went on, looking angrily at Alice. And a great many voices all said together ("like the chorus of a song," thought Alice) "Don't keep him waiting, child! Why, his time is worth a thousand pounds a minute!"

"I'm afraid I haven't got one," Alice said in a frightened tone: "there wasn't a ticket-office where I came from." And again the chorus of voices went on. "There wasn't room for one where she came from. The land there is worth a thousand pounds an inch!"[95]

"Don't make excuses," said the Guard: "you should have bought one from the engine-driver." And once more the chorus of voices went on with "The man that drives the engine. Why, the smoke alone is worth a thousand pounds a puff!"

Alice thought to herself "Then there's no use in speaking."[96] The voices didn't join in, *this* time, as she hadn't spoken, but, to her great surprise, they all *thought* in chorus (I hope you understand[97] what *thinking in chorus* means—for I must confess that *I* don't), "Better say nothing at all. Language is worth a thousand pounds a word!"

"I shall dream about a thousand pounds to-night, I know I shall!" thought Alice.

becomes obvious. And we have of course been fore-warned by the Queen's earlier directions.

95 From being rather antagonistic towards Alice, the "voices" now appear to be on her side.

96 *Then there's no use in speaking*—Alice's comment does not seem at all relevant to the situation.

97 *I hope you understand*—the second of the five instance of the author addressing the reader directly. In *Alice's Adventures in Wonderland*, he does so on four occasions.

All this time the Guard was looking at her, first through a telescope, then through a microscope,[98] and then through an opera-glass. At last he said "You're traveling the wrong way," and shut up the window, and went away.

"So young a child," said the gentleman sitting opposite to her, (he was dressed in white paper,) "ought to know which way she's going, even if she doesn't know her own name!"[99]

A Goat, that was sitting next to the gentleman in white, shut his eyes and said in a loud voice "She ought to know her way to the ticket-office, even if she doesn't know her alphabet!"[100]

98   *through a microscope*—this would be a tricky exercise, one might even say impossible.

99   We have been given no indication that Alice does not know her own name.

100   Again this is an unfair comment by the Goat—Alice had told the Guard

There was a Beetle[101] sitting next to the Goat (it was a very queer carriage-full of passengers altogether), and, as the rule seemed to be that they should all speak in turn, *he* went on with "She'll have to go back from here as luggage!"

Alice couldn't see who was sitting beyond the Beetle, but a hoarse voice spoke next. "Change engines——" it said, and there it choked and was obliged to leave off.

"It sounds like a horse," Alice thought to herself. And an extremely small voice, close to her ear, said 'You might make a joke on that—something about 'horse' and 'hoarse,' you know.'

Then a very gentle voice in the distance said "She must be labeled 'Lass, with care,' you know——"[102]

And after that other voices went on ("What a number of people there are in the carriage!" thought Alice), saying "She must go by post, as she's got a head on her——" "She must be sent as a message by the telegraph——" "She must draw the train herself the rest of the way——," and so on.

But the gentleman dressed in white paper leaned forwards and whispered in her ear "Never mind what they all say, my dear, but take a return-ticket every time the train stops."

"Indeed I sha'n't!" Alice said rather impatiently. "I don't belong to this railway journey at all—I was in a wood just now—and I wish I could get back there!"

'You might make a joke on *that*,' said the little voice close to her ear: 'something about 'you *would* if you could', you know.'[103]

---

that there was no ticket-office, not that she did not know her way there, and the accusation about the alphabet is quite unwarranted; he knows nothing of her alphabet skills.

101   Though we are not told, the Beetle must be huge—of equivalent size to the Goat and gentleman in white.

102   *"Lass, with care,"* as pointed out in *The Annotated Alice*, this is an in-joke, reminding us of glass objects being labeled "Glass, with care" when posted.

103   The inverted comma before 'you *would*' is incorrect, as the Gnat is using reported speech, not direct speech.

"Don't tease so," said Alice, looking about in vain to see where the voice came from. "If you're so anxious to have a joke made, why don't you make one yourself?"

The little voice sighed deeply. It was *very* unhappy, evidently, and Alice would have said something pitying to comfort it, "if it would only sigh like other people!" she thought. But this was such a wonderfully small sigh, that she wouldn't have heard it at all, if it hadn't come *quite* close to her ear. The consequence of this was that it tickled her ear very much, and quite took off her thoughts from the unhappiness of the poor little creature.[104]

'I know you are a friend,' the little voice went on: 'a dear friend and an old friend. And you wo'n't hurt me, though I *am* an insect.'

"What kind of insect?" Alice inquired, a little anxiously. What she really wanted to know was, whether it could sting or not, but she thought this wouldn't be quite a civil question to ask.

'What, then you don't—' the little voice began, when it was drowned by a shrill scream from the engine, and everybody jumped up in alarm, Alice among the rest.

The Horse,[105] who had put his head out of the window, quietly drew it in and said "It's only a brook we have to jump over." Everybody seemed satisfied with this, though Alice felt a little nervous at the idea of trains jumping at all. "However, it'll take us into the Fourth Square, that's some comfort!" she said to herself. In another moment she felt the carriage rise straight up into the air, and in her fright she caught at the thing nearest to her hand, which happened to be the Goat's beard.

---

104 *poor little creature*—Alice assumes it is a creature of some sort, though she has no idea, yet, as to what it might be.

105 Our author confirms that it is indeed a horse that is in the carriage—confirming Alice's earlier conjecture—and also making the gnat's suggested joke a reasonable suggestion.

*106

But the beard seemed to melt away as she touched it, and she found herself sitting quietly under a tree—while the Gnat (for that was the insect she had been talking to) was balancing itself on a twig just over her head, and fanning her with its wings.

It certainly was a *very* large Gnat: "about the size of a chicken," Alice thought.[107] Still, she couldn't feel nervous with it, after they had been talking together so long.

"—then you don't like *all* insects?" the Gnat went on, as quietly as if nothing had happened.[108]

"I like them when they can talk," Alice said. "None of them ever talk, where *I* come from."

"What sort of insects do you rejoice in, where *you* come from?" the Gnat inquired.

"I don't *rejoice* in[109] insects at all," Alice explained, "because I'm rather afraid of them—at least the large kinds. But I can tell you the names of some of them."

"Of course they answer to their names?" the Gnat remarked carelessly.

106 The asterisks here denote the second half of Alice's double move as Pawn to Queen's 4 (Alice d2–d3), the second "jump" by the train indicating the second half.

107 *a VERY large Gnat*—the Gnat does appear to have increased hugely in size. Apart from the later development of characters in the hearth of Looking-Glass House, this is the only instance of a character changing size in the whole book, unlike *Wonderland* where such changes are a common occurrence.

108 The Gnat is repeating the question it had started just before the train jump.

109 *rejoice in*—the Gnat is using an acceptable phrase. It is Alice, who may not have met this use before, who takes exception to it.

"I never knew them do it."

"What's the use of their having names," the Gnat said, "if they wo'n't answer to them?"

"No use to *them*," said Alice; "but it's useful to the people that name them, I suppose. If not, why do things have names at all?"

"I ca'n't say," the Gnat replied. "Further on, in the wood down there, they've got no names[110]—however, go on with your list of insects: you're wasting time."

"Well, there's the Horse-fly," Alice began, counting off the names on her fingers.

"All right," said the Gnat. "Half way up that bush, you'll see a Rocking-horse-fly, if you look. It's made entirely of wood, and gets about by swinging itself from branch to branch."

"What does it live on?" Alice asked, with great curiosity.

"Sap and sawdust," said the Gnat. "Go on with the list."

Alice looked at the Rocking-horse-fly with great interest, and made up her mind it must have been just repainted, it looked so bright and sticky; and then she went on.

"And there's the Dragon-fly."

110   The Gnat does not clarify whether it is talking about there being no names for insects in the wood, or names in general. Things will be clarified in due course.

"Look on the branch above your head," said the Gnat, "and there you'll find a Snap-dragon-fly. Its body in made of plum-pudding, its wings of holly-leaves, and its head is a raisin burning in brandy."

"And what does it live on?" Alice asked, as before.

"Frumenty and mince-pie," the Gnat replied; "and it makes its nest in a Christmas-box."

"And then there's the Butterfly," Alice went on, after she had taken a good look at the insect with its head on fire, and had thought to herself "I wonder if that's the reason insects are so fond of flying into candles—because they want to turn into Snap-dragon-flies!"

"Crawling at your feet," said the Gnat (Alice drew her feet back in some alarm), "you may observe a Bread-and-butter-fly. It swings are thin slices of bread-and-butter, its body is a crust, and its head is a lump of sugar."

"And what does *it* live on?"

"Weak tea with cream in it."

A new difficulty came into Alice's head. "Supposing it couldn't find any?" she suggested.

"Then it would die, of course."

"But that must happen very often," Alice remarked thoughtfully.

"It always happens," said the Gnat.[111]

After this, Alice was silent for a minute or two, pondering. The Gnat amused itself meanwhile by humming round and round her head: at last it settled again and remarked "I suppose you don't want to lose your name?"

"No, indeed," Alice said, a little anxiously.

"And yet I don't know," the Gnat went on in a careless tone: "only think how convenient it would be if you could manage to go home without it! For instance, if the governess wanted to call you to your lessons,[112] she would call out 'Come here——,' and there she would have to leave off, because there wouldn't be any name for her to call, and of course you wouldn't have to go, you know."

"That would never do, I'm sure," said Alice: "the governess would never think of excusing me lessons for that. If she couldn't remember my name, she'd call me 'Miss,' as the servants do."[113]

---

111 This is the first and only death reference in the book—though Humpty Dumpty does refer to "leaving off at seven", and to his possible fall (as we shall see below)—a very different situation to that pertaining in *Wonderland*.

112 The Gnat recognizes Alice as being upper middle class, and taught by a governess, rather than a child who attends a school.

113 With the reference to servants, Alice confirms her middle class status.

"Well, if she said 'Miss,' and didn't say anything more," the Gnat remarked, "of course you'd miss your lessons. That's a joke. I wish *you* had made it."[114]

"Why do you wish *I* had made it?" Alice asked. "It's a very bad one."

But the Gnat only sighed more deeply, while two large tears came rolling down its cheeks.[115]

"You shouldn't make jokes," Alice said, "if it makes you so unhappy."

Then came another of those melancholy little sighs, and this time the poor Gnat really seemed to have sighed itself away, for, when Alice looked up, there was nothing whatever to be seen on the twig,[116] and, as she was getting quite chilly with sitting so long, she got up and walked on.

She very soon came to an open field, with a wood on the other side of it:[117] it looked much darker than the last wood, and Alice felt a *little* timid about going into it. However, on second thoughts, she made up her mind to go on: "for I certainly wo'n't go *back*," she thought to herself, and this was the only way to the Eighth Square.

"This must be the wood," she said thoughtfully to herself, "where things have no names. I wonder what'll become of *my* name when I go in? I shouldn't like to lose it at all——because they'd have to give me another, and it would almost certainly be an ugly one. But then the fun would be,

---

114   This reminds us of the earlier comments by the Gnat while they were in the railway carriage, where it keeps suggesting jokes that Alice could make.

115   An authorial comment which emphasizes the anthropomorphism of the Gnat.

116   This is the second time in the book that a character has suddenly vanished (the other being the Red Queen at the end of Chapter II).

117   Four different woods feature in the book—here, with the Tweedles, with the White Knight, and during her conversation with the White Knight, she refers to "the last wood" which she says was "much darker than this wood"—though quite what wood that was is not vouchsafed to us.

trying to find the creature that had got my old name![118]
That's just like the advertisements, you know, when people
lose dogs——'answers to the name of "Dash": had on a brass
collar'——just fancy calling everything you met 'Alice' till
one of them answered! Only they wouldn't answer at all, if
they were wise."

She was rambling on in this way when she reached the
wood: it looked very cool and shady. "Well, at any rate it's a
great comfort," she said as she stepped under the trees,
"after being so hot, to get into the—into the—into *what*?"
she went on, rather surprised at not being able to think of the
word. "I mean to get under the—under the—under *this*, you
know!" putting her hand on the trunk of the tree. "What *does*
it call itself, I wonder?[119] I do believe it's got no name—why,
to be sure it hasn't!"

She stood silent for a minute, thinking: then she suddenly
began again. "Then it really *has* happened, after all! And
now, who am I? I *will* remember, if I can! I'm determined to
do it!" But being determined didn't help her much,[120] and all
she could say, after a great deal of puzzling, was "L, I *know*
it begins with L!"

Just then a Fawn came wandering by: it looked at Alice
with its large gentle eyes, but didn't seem at all frightened.
"Here then! Here then!" Alice said, as she held out her hand
and tried to stroke it; but it only started back a little, and
then stood looking at her again.

"What do you call yourself?" the Fawn said at last. Such a
soft sweet voice it had!

"I wish I knew!" thought poor Alice. She answered, rather
sadly, "Nothing, just now."

---

118 Alice makes the quite unwarranted assumption that a name is so dynamic
that if she lost it, it would automatically go to another person.

119 *"What DOES it call itself*—a whimsical idea that the tree can talk to itself.

120 *didn't help her much*—of course, it didn't help at all.

"Think again," it said: "that wo'n't do."

Alice thought, but nothing came of it. "Please, would you tell me what *you* call yourself?" she said timidly. "I think that might help a little."

"I'll tell you, if you'll come a little further on," the Fawn said. "I ca'n't remember *here*."[121]

So they walked on together through the wood, Alice with her arms clasped lovingly around the soft neck of the Fawn, till they came out into another open field, and here the Fawn gave a sudden bound into the air, and shook itself free from Alice's arm. "I'm a Fawn!" it cried out in a voice of delight.

121   *I ca'n't remember here*—the Fawn apparently knows there is a problem in the wood, so it is a little odd that it suggests that if Alice tries harder, she *will* be able to overcome the problem.

"And, dear me! You're a human child!"[122] A sudden look of alarm came into its beautiful brown eyes, and in another moment it had darted away at full speed.

Alice stood looking after it, almost ready to cry with vexation at having lost her dear little fellow-traveler so suddenly. "However, I know my name now," she said: "that's *some* comfort. Alice—Alice—I wo'n't forget it again. And now, which of these finger-posts ought I to follow, I wonder?"

It was not a very difficult question to answer, and there was only one road through the wood, and the two finger-posts both pointed along it. "I'll settle it," Alice said to herself, "when the road divides and they point different ways."

But this did not seem likely to happen. She went on and on, a long way, but, wherever the road divided, there were sure to be two finger-posts pointing the same way, one marked "TO TWEEDLEDUMS'S HOUSE," and the other "TO THE HOUSE OF TWEEDLEDEE."

"I do believe," said Alice at last, "that they live in the *same* house! I wonder I never thought of that before—but I ca'n't stay there long. I'll just call and say 'How d'ye do?' and ask them the way out of the wood.[123] If I could only get to the Eighth Square before it gets dark!" So she wandered on, talking to herself as she went, till, on turning a sharp corner, she came upon two fat little men, so suddenly that she could not help starting back, but in another moment she recovered herself, feeling sure that they must be

---

122   It is interesting that the Fawn only reacts to Alice with alarm once it knows the "name"—even though it has seen her quite clearly up to now.

123   *the way out of the wood*—with the Fawn she had just emerged from a wood into an open field—so she has now entered another wood.

INTRODUCTION TO CHAPTER IV

The last chapter finished without a full stop—so that the last phrase and the next chapter title form a rhyming couplet. The stop was absent until the 1897 revision was made for the 61st Thousand, when it was, mistakenly in my view, added. The new chapter is unique in the Alice books in that she meets two boys, the only time she meets any other children (apart from the Duchess's baby!). She copes admirably with two argumentative and wayward characters.

CHAPTER IV

Tweedledum and Tweedledee

*T*hey were standing under a tree, each with an arm round the other's neck, and Alice knew which was which in a moment, because one of them had "DUM" embroidered on his collar, and the other "DEE." "I suppose they've each got 'TWEEDLE' round at the back of the collar," she said to herself.[124]

They stood so still that she quite forgot they were alive, and she was just going round to see if the word "TWEEDLE" was written at the back of each collar, when she was startled by a voice coming from the one marked "DUM."

"If you think we're wax-works," he said, "you ought to pay, you know. Wax-works weren't made to be looked at for nothing. Nohow!"[125]

124 As pointed out in *The Annotated Alice*, the words are not reversed as one might have expected in Looking-Glass land.

125 *Nohow*—is the first neologism in the book, it implies a negative reaction.

"Contrariwise," added the one marked "DEE," "if you think we're alive, you ought to speak."[126]

"I'm sure I'm very sorry," was all Alice could say; for the words of the old song kept ringing through her head like the ticking of a clock, and she could hardly help saying them out loud:—[127]

"Tweedledum and Tweedledee
Agreed to have a battle;
For Tweedledum said Tweedledee
Had spoiled his nice new rattle.

Just then flew down a monstrous crow,
As black as a tar-barrel;
Which frightened both the heroes so,
They quite forgot their quarrel."

"I know what you're thinking about," said Tweedledum; "but it isn't so, nohow."

"Contrariwise," continued Tweedledee, "if it was so, it might be; and if it were so, it would be; but as it isn't, it ain't. That's logic."[128]

On the other hand *Contrariwise*, while being very unusual, was a word in Victorian England, and which Tweedledee is using correctly—as meaning 'on the contrary'. Both brothers however appear to use the words simply as expletives, except for this one instance where Tweedledee is using "contrariwise" in its usual meaning.

126 *if you think we're alive, you ought to speak*—the Tweedles have the option of opening the conversation themselves, but choose not to do so.

127 The fact that the well known nursery rhyme comes into her head, could confirm the suspicion that they might indeed be wax-works—i.e. models designed to illustrate the poem.

128 In the various dialogues in this encounter, Tweedledum is the primary

"I was thinking," Alice said very politely, "which is the best way out of this wood: it's getting so dark. Would you tell me, please?"

But the fat little men only looked at each other and grinned.

They looked so exactly like a couple of great schoolboys, that Alice couldn't help pointing her finger at Tweedledum, and saying "First Boy!"

"Nohow!" Tweedledum cried out briskly, and shut his mouth up again with a snap.

"Next Boy!" said Alice, passing on to Tweedledee, though she felt quite certain he would only shout "Contrariwise!" and so he did.

spokesperson, with Tweedledee following up, as it were. Their argument here is belied by what is to come, when the poem is indeed acted out in full.

"You've begun wrong!" cried Tweedledum. "The first thing in a visit is to say 'How d'ye do?'[129] and shake hands!" And here the two brothers gave each other a hug, and then they held out the two hands that were free, to shake hands with her.

Alice did not like shaking hands with either of them first, for fear of hurting the other one's feelings; so, as the best way out of the difficulty, she took hold of both hands at once: the next moment they were dancing round in a ring. This seemed quite natural (she remembered afterwards), and she was not even surprised to hear music playing: it seemed to come from the tree under which they were dancing, and it was done (as well as she could make out) by the branches rubbing one across the other, like fiddles and fiddle-sticks.

"But it certainly *was* funny," (Alice said afterwards, when she was telling her sister[130] the history of all this,) "to find myself singing '*Here we go round the mulberry bush.*' I don't know when I began it, but somehow I felt as if I had been singing it a long long time!"

The other two dancers were fat, and very soon out of breath. "Four times round is enough for one dance," Tweedledum panted out, and they left off dancing as suddenly as they had begun: the music stopped at the same moment.

Then they let go of Alice's hands, and stood looking at her for a minute: there was a rather awkward pause, as Alice didn't know how to begin a conversation with people she had just been dancing with. "It would never do to say 'How d'ye

---

129   *say 'How d'ye do?'*—this is exactly what Alice had intended to do in her soliloquy at the end of Chapter III.

130   *telling her sister*—this would appear to be the elder sister, who played such a prominent role in *Alice's Adventures in Wonderland*, rather than the younger (?) sister who is mentioned in Chapter I.

do?' *now*," she said to herself: "we seem to have got beyond that, somehow!"

"I hope you're not much tired?" she said at last.[131]

"Nohow. And thank you *very* much for asking," said Tweedledum.

"So *much* obliged!"[132] added Tweedledee. "You like poetry?"

"Ye-es, pretty well—*some* poetry," Alice said doubtfully. "Would you tell me which road leads out of the wood?"[133]

"What shall I repeat to her?" said Tweedledee, looking round at Tweedledum with great solemn eyes, and not noticing Alice's question.

"'*The Walrus and the Carpenter*' is the longest," Tweedledum replied, giving his brother an affectionate hug.

Tweedledee began instantly:—

> *"The sun was shining——"*

Here Alice ventured to interrupt him. "If it's *very* long," she said, as politely as she could, "would you please tell me first which road——"

Tweedledee smiled gently, and began again:—

> *"The sun was shining on the sea,*
> *Shining with all his might:*
> *He did his very best to make*
> *The billows smooth and bright—*
> *And this was odd, because it was*
> *The middle of the night.*

---

131 Alice is again ready to take the initiative to restart the conversation.

132 The only occasion in this chapter, where Tweedledee does *not* say "Contrariwise" after his brother's "Nohow".

133 It was established earlier that she was on the one road—with the two signs. One must assume that she can now see a choice ahead.

The moon was shining sulkily,
 Because she thought the sun
Had got no business to be there
 After the day was done—
'It's very rude of him,' she said,
 'To come and spoil the fun!"

The sea was wet as wet could be,
 The sands were dry as dry.
You could not see a cloud, because
 No cloud was in the sky:
No birds were flying overhead—
 There were no birds to fly.

The Walrus and the Carpenter
 Were walking close at hand:
They wept like anything to see
 Such quantities of sand:
'If this were only cleared away,'
 They said, 'it would be grand!'

'If seven maids with seven mops
Swept it for half a year,
Do you suppose,' the Walrus said,
'That they would get it clear?'
'I doubt it,' said the Carpenter,
And shed a bitter tear.[134]

'O Oysters, come and walk with us!'
The Walrus did beseech.
'A pleasant walk, a pleasant talk,
Along the briny beach:
We cannot do with more than four,
To give a hand to each.'

The eldest Oyster looked at him,
But never a word he said:
The eldest Oyster winked his eye,
And shook his heavy head—
Meaning to say he did not choose
To leave the oyster-bed.

But four young Oysters hurried up,
All eager for the treat:
Their coats were brushed, their faces washed,
Their shoes were clean and neat—
And this was odd, because, you know,
They hadn't any feet.

---

134 *And shed a bitter tear*—in addition to the tears they were already shedding (verse 4)?

Four other Oysters followed them,
And yet another four;
And think and fast they came at last,
And more, and more, and more—
All hopping through the frothy waves,
And scrambling to the shore.

The Walrus and the Carpenter
Walked on a mile or so,
And then they rested on a rock
Conveniently low:
And all the little Oysters stood
And waited in a row.

'The time has come,' the Walrus said,
'To talk of many things:
Of shoes—and ships—and sealing wax—
Of cabbages—and kings—
And why the sea is boiling hot—
And whether pigs have wings.'

'But wait a bit,' the Oysters cried,
  'Before we have our chat;
For some of us are out of breath,
  And all of us are fat!'
'No hurry!' said the Carpenter.
  They thanked him much for that.

'A loaf of bread,' the Walrus said,
  'Is what we chiefly need:
Pepper and vinegar besides
  Are very good indeed—
Now, if you're ready, Oysters dear,
  We can begin to feed.'

'But not on us!' the Oysters cried,
  Turning a little blue,[135]
'After such kindness, that would be
  A dismal thing to do!'
'The night is fine,' the Walrus said,
  'Do you admire the view?

'It was so kind of you to come!
  And you are very nice!'
The Carpenter said nothing but
  'Cut us another slice.
I wish you were not quite so deaf—
  I've had to ask you twice!'[136]

---

135 *Turning a little blue*—a little tricky for oysters.

136 *I've had to ask you twice*—*we* have only heard the second request.

'It seems a shame,' the Walrus said,
  'To play them such a trick,
After we've brought them out so far,
  And made them trot so quick!'
The Carpenter said nothing but
  'The butter's spread too thick!'

'I weep for you,'[137] the Walrus said:
  'I deeply sympathize,'
With sobs and tears he sorted out
  Those of the largest size,
Holding his pocket-handkerchief
  Before his streaming eyes.

---

137 *I weep for you*—is the Walrus sympathizing with the Carpenter about the
     butter being spread too thick? It is rather more likely (and confirmed by the
     later conversation), that he is expressing ironic sympathy for the fate of the
     oysters.

'O Oysters,' said the Carpenter,
'You've had a pleasant run!
Shall we be trotting home again?'
But answer came there none—
And this was scarcely odd, because
They'd eaten every one."

"I like the Walrus best,"[138] said Alice: "because he was a *little* sorry for the poor oysters."

"He ate more than the Carpenter, though," said Tweedledee. "You see he held his handkerchief in front, so that the Carpenter couldn't count how many he took: contrariwise."[139]

"That was mean!" Alice said indignantly. "Then I like the Carpenter best—if he didn't eat as many as the Walrus."

"But he ate as many as he could get," said Tweedledum.[140]

This was a puzzler. After a pause, Alice began "Well! They were *both* very unpleasant characters——" here she checked herself in some alarm, at hearing something that sounded to her like the puffing of a large steam-engine in the wood near them, though she feared it was more likely to be a wild beast. "Are there any lions or tigers about here?" she asked timidly.

"It's only the Red King snoring," said Tweedledee.

"Come and look at him!" the brothers cried, and they each took one of Alice's hands, and led her up to where the King was sleeping.

"Isn't he a *lovely* sight?" said Tweedledum.

Alice couldn't honestly say that he was. He had a tall red night-cap on, with a tassel, and he was lying crumpled up

138 *best*—Alice should really have said "better", as there are only two characters that she is judging—but one must not be pedantic.

139 *contrariwise*—the second occasion where Tweedledee uses the word not as an expletive, but as part of his argument.

140 Both Tweedles are giving us information that was not in the original poem.

into a sort of untidy heap, and snoring loud——"fit to snore his head off!" as Tweedledum remarked.

"I'm afraid he'll catch cold with lying on the damp grass," said Alice, who was a very thoughtful little girl.

"He's dreaming now," said Tweedledee: "and what do you think he's dreaming about?"

Alice said "Nobody can guess that."

"Why, about *you*!" Tweedledee exclaimed, clapping his hands triumphantly. "And if he left off dreaming about you, where do you suppose you'd be?"[141]

"Where I am now, of course," said Alice.

Not you!" Tweedledee retorted contemptuously. "You'd be nowhere. Why, you're only a sort of thing in his dream!"

"If that there King was to wake," added Tweedledum, "you'd go out—bang!—Just like a candle!"

141 Alice is of course quite right—they could not possibly know what he was dreaming about, and to dream about Alice is very unlikely in that the Red King has never met her, so knows nothing about her whatever. Curiously, after this "meeting" the Red King is never mentioned again throughout the entire book.

"I shouldn't!" Alice exclaimed indignantly. "Besides, if *I'm* only a sort of thing in his dream, what are *you*, I should like to know?"

"Ditto," said Tweedledum.

"Ditto, ditto!" cried Tweedledee.[142]

He shouted this so loud that Alice couldn't help saying "Hush! You'll be waking him, I'm afraid, if you make so much noise."

"Well, it's no use *your* talking about waking him," said Tweedledum, "when you're only one of the things in his dream. You know very well you're not real."[143]

"I *am* real!" said Alice, and began to cry.

"You wo'n't make yourself a bit realler by crying," Tweedledee remarked: "there's nothing to cry about."

"If I wasn't real," Alice said—half-laughing through her tears, it all seemed so ridiculous—"I shouldn't be able to cry."

"I hope you don't suppose those are *real* tears?" Tweedledum interrupted in a tone of great contempt.

"I know they're talking nonsense," Alice thought to herself: "and it's foolish to cry about it." So she brushed away her tears, and went on, as cheerfully as she could, "At any rate I'd better be getting on out of the wood, for really it's coming on very dark. Do you think it's going to rain?"

Tweedledum spread a large umbrella over himself and his brother, and looked up into it. "No, I don't think it is," he said: "at least—not under *here*. Nohow."

---

142 These comments do not make it clear as to whether the brothers are agreeing with Alice, or disagreeing with her, as they do not answer her question.

143 This does now clarify that the brothers have not agreed with Alice's suggestion that they also might be "things" in the King's dream. And there is a certain arrogance in Tweedledum's comment that Alice "knows very well" that she is not real—he assumes she has accepted the suggestion—which we know she has not.

"But it may rain *outside*?"

"It may—if it chooses," said Tweedledee: "we've no objection. Contrariwise."

"Selfish things!" thought Alice, and she was just going to say "Goodnight" and leave them, when Tweedledum sprang out from under the umbrella, and seized her by the wrist.

"Do you see *that*?" he said, in a voice choking with passion, and his eyes grew larger and yellow all in a moment, as he pointed with a trembling finger at a small white thing lying under the tree.

"It's only a rattle," Alice said, after a careful examination of the little white thing. "Not a rattle-*snake*, you know," she added hastily, thinking that he was frightened: "only an old rattle—quite old and broken."[144]

"I knew it was!" cried Tweedledum, beginning to stamp about wildly and tear his hair. "It's spoilt, of course!" Here he looked at Tweedledee, who immediately sat down on the ground, and tried to hide himself under the umbrella.

---

144 Alice asserts that not only is it broken, but it is also "quite old". One can understand it being broken, but why, if bought yesterday, does it look old— within 24 hours of purchase?

Alice laid her hand upon his arm, and said, in a soothing tone, "You needn't be so angry about an old rattle."

"But it *isn't* old!" Tweedledum cried, in a greater fury than ever. "It's *new*, I tell you—I bought it yesterday—my nice NEW RATTLE!" and his voice rose to a perfect scream.

All this time Tweedledee was trying his best to fold up the umbrella, with himself in it: which was such an extraordinary thing to do, that it quite took off Alice's attention from the angry brother. But he couldn't quite succeed, and it ended in his rolling over, bundled up in the umbrella, with only his head out: and there he lay, opening and shutting his mouth and his large eyes——"looking more like a fish than anything else," Alice thought.

"Of course you agree to have a battle?" Tweedledum said in a calmer tone.

"I suppose so," the other sulkily replied, as he crawled out of the umbrella: "only *she* must help us to dress up, you know."

So the two brothers went off hand-in-hand into the wood, and returned in a minute with their arms full of things— such as bolsters, blankets, hearth-rugs, table-cloths, dish-covers, and coal-scuttles. "I hope you're good hand at pinning and tying strings?" Tweedledum remarked. "Every one of these things has got to go on, somehow or other."[145]

Alice said afterwards that she had never seen such a fuss made about anything in all her life—the way those two bustled about—and the quantity of things they put on—and the trouble they gave her in tying strings and fastening buttons——"Really they'll be more like bundles of old clothes than anything else, by the time they're ready!" she said to herself, as she arranged a bolster round the neck of

---

145 If a third party is needed to help putting things on, one wonders how they cope when on their own (presuming that they have had battles before, which seems likely).

Tweedledee, "to keep his head from being cut off," as he said.[146]

"You know," he added very gravely, "it's one of the most serious things that can possibly happen to one in a battle—to get one's head cut off."

Alice laughed loud: but she managed to turn it into a cough, for fear of hurting his feelings.

"Do I look very pale?" said Tweedledum, coming up to have his helmet tied on. (He *called* it a helmet, though it certainly looked much more like a saucepan.)

"Well yes—a *little*," Alice replied gently.

"I'm very brave, generally," he went on in a low voice: "only to-day I happen to have a headache."

"And *I've* got a toothache!" said Tweedledee, who had overheard the remark. "I'm far worse than you!"

---

146 *to keep his head from being cut off*—the use of "his head" rather than "my head" suggests this is reported speech, so the inverted commas are in fact incorrect.

"Then you'd better not fight to-day," said Alice, thinking it a good opportunity to make peace.

"We *must* have a bit of a fight, but I don't care about going on long," said Tweedledum. "What's the time now?"

Tweedledee looked at his watch, and said "Half-past four."

"Let's fight till six, and then have dinner," said Tweedledum.

"Very well," the other said, rather sadly: "and *she* can watch us—only you'd better not come *very* close," he added: "I generally hit every thing I can see—when I get really excited."

"And *I* hit every thing within reach," cried Tweedledum, "whether I can see it or not!"

Alice laughed, "You must hit the *trees* pretty often, I should think," she said.

Tweedledum looked round him with a satisfied smile. "I don't suppose," he said, "there'll be a tree left standing, for ever so far round, by the time we've finished!"

"And all about a rattle!" said Alice, still hoping to make them a *little* ashamed of fighting for such a trifle.

"I shouldn't have minded it so much," said Tweedledum, "if it hadn't been a new one."

"I wish the monstrous crow would come!" thought Alice.[147]

"There's only one sword, you know," Tweedledum said to his brother: "but *you* can have the umbrella—it's quite as sharp. Only we must begin quick.[148] It's getting as dark as it can."

"And darker," said Tweedledee.

---

147 This is the first intimation that Alice appreciates that the poem about the Tweedles is in the process of being acted out. The brothers appear to be totally unaware of this.

148 *begin quick*—one would expect "begin quickly"—but they are boys, so a lapse in grammar is permissible?

It was getting dark so suddenly that Alice thought there must be a thunderstorm coming on. "What a thick black cloud that is!" she said. "And how fast it comes! Why, I do believe it's got wings!"[149]

"It's the crow!" Tweedledum cried out in a shrill voice of alarm; and the two brothers took to their heels and were out of sight in a moment.[150]

Alice ran a little way into the wood, and stopped under a large tree. "It can never get at me *here*," she thought: "it's far too large to squeeze itself in among the trees. But I wish it wouldn't flap its wings so—it makes quite a hurricane in the wood—here's somebody's shawl being blown away!"

---

149   For the moment Alice seems to have forgotten the possibility of the crow arriving.

150   In a curious reversal—now the Tweedles suddenly appreciate that the crow has arrived. Their swift departure does not appear to be impeded by the amount of extra items they are wearing.

INTRODUCTION TO CHAPTER V

*A*s with other chapter endings, Chapter IV ends with Alice alone, and in a somewhat dramatic situation. The shawl gives us an idea of what is about to happen. We meet the White Queen for the first time—a remarkably different character from her Red counterpart. We see Alice in a new light—almost motherly.

C H A P T E R   V

Wool and Water

She caught the shawl as she spoke, and looked about for the owner: in another moment the White Queen came running wildly through the wood, with both arms stretched out wide, as if she were flying, and Alice very civilly went to meet her with the shawl.

"I'm very glad I happened to be in the way," Alice said, as she helped her to put on her shawl again.

The White Queen only looked at her in a helpless frightened sort of way, and kept repeating something in a whisper to herself that sounded like "Bread-and-butter, bread-and-butter," and Alice felt that if there was to be any conversation at all, she must manage it herself. So she began rather timidly: "Am I addressing the White Queen?"

"Well, yes, if you call that a-dressing," the Queen said. "It isn't *my* notion of the thing at all."[151]

---

151   The Queen of course is misinterpreting Alice's way of describing her opening remark, for the process of putting on clothes etc. Alice, as a polite little girl immediately adopts the Queen's understanding.

Alice thought it would never do to have an argument at the very beginning of their conversation, so she smiled and said "If your Majesty will only tell me the right way to begin, I'll do it as well as I can."

"But I don't want it done at all!" groaned the poor Queen. "I've been a-dressing myself for the last two hours."

It would have been all the better, as it seemed to Alice, if she had got some one else to dress her, she was so dreadfully untidy. "Every single thing's crooked," Alice thought to herself, "and she's all over pins!——May I put your shawl straight for you?" she added aloud.

"I don't know what's the matter with it!" the Queen said, in a melancholy voice. "It's out of temper, I think. I've pinned it here, and I've pinned it there, but there's no pleasing it!"

"It *ca'n't* go straight, you know, if you pin it all on one side," Alice said, as she gently put it right for her; "and, dear me, what a state your hair is in!"

"The brush has got entangled in it!" the Queen said with a sigh. "And I lost the comb yesterday."

Alice carefully released the brush, and did her best to get the hair into order. "Come, you look rather better now!" she said, after altering most of the pins. "But really you should have a lady's-maid!"

"I'm sure I'll take *you* with pleasure!" the Queen said. "Twopence a week, and jam every other day."

Alice couldn't help laughing, as she said "I don't want you to hire *me*—and I don't care for jam."[152]

"It's very good jam," said the Queen.

"Well, I don't want any *to-day*, at any rate."

"You couldn't have it you *did* want it," the Queen said. "The rule is, jam to-morrow and jam yesterday—but never jam *to-day*."

152　A slight change in Alice's preferences from *Wonderland*, where Alice looked forward to the jam tarts being handed round at the end of the trial.

"It *must* come sometimes to 'jam to-day,'" Alice objected.

"No, it ca'n't," said the Queen, "It's jam every *other* day: to-day isn't any *other* day, you know."

"I don't understand you," said Alice. "It's dreadfully confusing!"[153]

"That's the effect of living backwards," the Queen said kindly: "it always makes one a little giddy at first——"[154]

"Living backwards!" Alice repeated in great astonishment. "I never heard of such a thing!"[155]

153 We all share Alice's confusion—a result of the Queen's strange way of playing with words.

154 The Queen's answer, of course, has nothing to do with living backwards. It is interesting that she recognizes that Alice comes from a different place, where living forward is the norm.

155 Alice has forgotten the problems she encountered earlier over how to reach the top of the hill, when about to meet the Red Queen.

"—but there's one great advantage in it. That one's memory works both ways."

"I'm sure *mine* only works one way," Alice remarked. "I ca'n't remember things before they happen."

"It's a poor sort of memory that only works backwards," the Queen remarked.

"What sort of things do *you* remember best?" Alice ventured to ask.

"Oh, things that happened the week after next,"[156] the Queen replied in a careless tone. "For instance, now," she went on, sticking a large piece of plaster on her finger as she spoke, "there's the King's Messenger. He's in prison now,

156 *Oh, things that happened the week after next*—the problems are neatly exposed in this unique way of having the word 'happened' in the past tense, when referring to the future.

being punished: and the trial doesn't even begin till next Wednesday: and of course the crime comes last of all."

"Suppose he never commits the crime?" said Alice.

"That would be all the better, wouldn't it?" the Queen said, as she bound the plaster round her finger with a bit of ribbon.[157]

Alice felt there was no denying *that*. "Of course it would be all the better," she said: "but it wouldn't be all the better his being punished."

"You're wrong *there*, at any rate," said the Queen. "Where *you* ever punished?"

"Only for faults," said Alice.

And you were all the better for it, I know!" the Queen said triumphantly.

"Yes, but then I *had* done the things I was punished for," said Alice: "that makes all the difference."

"But if you *hadn't* done them," the Queen said, "that would have been better still; better, and better, and better!" Her voice went higher with each "better," till it got quite to a squeak at last.

Alice was just beginning to say "There's a mistake somewhere———," when the Queen began screaming, so loud that she had to leave the sentence unfinished. "Oh, oh, oh!" shouted the Queen, shaking he hand about as if she wanted to shake it off. "My finger's bleeding! Oh, oh, oh, oh!"

Her screams were so exactly like the whistle of a steam-engine, that Alice had to hold both her hands over her ears.

"What *is* the matter?" she said, as soon as there was a chance of making herself heard. "Have you pricked your finger?"

"I haven't pricked it *yet*," the Queen said, "but I soon shall—oh, oh, oh!"

---

157 The drama of the ongoing situation is nicely accentuated by Alice not noticing what the Queen is doing with her finger, during this conversation.

"When do you expect to do it?" Alice asked, feeling very much inclined to laugh.

"When I fasten my shawl again," the poor Queen groaned out: "the brooch will come undone directly. Oh, oh!" As she said the words, the brooch flew open, and the Queen clutched wildly at it, and tried to clasp it again.

"Take care!" cried Alice. "You're holding it all crooked!" And she caught at the brooch; but it was too late: the pin had slipped, and the Queen had pricked her finger.

"That accounts for the bleeding, you see," she said to Alice with a smile. "Now you understand the way things happen here."

"But why don't you scream *now?*" Alice asked, holding her hands ready to put over her ears again.

"Why, I've done all the screaming already," said the Queen. "What would be the good of having it all over again?"

By this time it was getting light. "The crow must have flown away, I think," said Alice: "I'm so glad it's gone. I thought it was the night coming on."

"I wish *I* could manage to be glad!" the Queen said. "Only I can never remember the rule. You must be very happy, living in this wood,[158] and being glad whenever you like!"

"Only it is so *very* lonely here!" Alice said in a melancholy voice; and, at the thought of her loneliness, two large tears came rolling down her cheeks.[159]

"Oh, don't go on like that!" cried the poor Queen, wringing her hands in despair. "Consider what a great girl you are.

---

158 *living in this wood*—the Queen has forgotten that Alice does not live in Looking-Glass land, and she is assuming she lives there purely because this is where they met.

159 We know all about Alice's "large tears" from her experiences in Wonderland.

Consider what a long way you've come to-day.[160] Consider what o'clock it is. Consider anything, only don't cry!"

Alice could not help laughing at this, even in the midst of her tears. "Can *you* keep from crying by considering things?" she asked.

"That's the way it's done," the Queen said with great decision: "nobody can do two things at once, you know. Let's consider your age to begin with——how old are you?"

"I'm seven and a half, exactly."

"You needn't say 'exactually,'"[161] the Queen remarked. "I can believe it without that. Now I'll give *you* something to believe. I'm just one hundred and one, five months and a day."

"I ca'n't believe *that!*" said Alice.

"Ca'n't you?" the Queen said in a pitying tone. "Try again: draw a long breath, and shut your eyes."

Alice laughed. "There's no use trying," she said: "one *ca'n't* believe in impossible things."

"I dare say you haven't had much practice," said the Queen. "When I was your age, I always did it for half-an-hour a day. Why, sometimes I've believed as many as six impossible things before breakfast. There goes the shawl again!"

The brooch had come undone as she spoke, and a sudden gust of wind blew the Queen's shawl across a little brook. The Queen spread out her arms again, and went flying after it, and this time she succeeded in catching it for herself. "I've

160 *Consider what a long way you've come to-day*—this is pure speculation by the Queen, she has no idea where Alice has come from, although from earlier in the conversation, she does understand that Alice does not live in Looking-Glass land, but even then she has a tendency to forget (as detailed just above).

161 *exactually*—a Carroll portmanteau word—from "exactly" and "actually". The Queen is responding to the "actually" part of the word which implies a certainty in Alice's statement.

got it!" she cried in a triumphant tone. "Now you shall see me pin it on again, all by myself!"

"Then I hope your finger is better now?" Alice said very politely,[162] as she crossed the little brook after the Queen.

"Oh, much better!" cried the Queen, her voice rising into a squeak as she went on. "Much be-etter! Be-etter! Be-e-e-etter! Be-e-ehh!" The last word ended in a long bleat, so like a sheep that Alice quite started.

She looked at the Queen, who seemed to have suddenly wrapped herself up in wool. Alice rubbed her eyes, and looked again. She couldn't make out what had happened at all. Was she in a shop? And was that really—was it really a *sheep* that was sitting on the other side of the counter? Rub as she would, she could make nothing more of it: she was in a little dark shop, leaning with her elbows on the counter, and opposite to her was an old Sheep, sitting in an arm-chair, knitting, and every now and then leaving off to look at her through a great pair of spectacles.[163]

"What is it you want to buy?" the Sheep said at last, looking up for a moment from her knitting.

"I don't *quite* know yet," Alice said very gently. "I should like to look all round me first, if I might."

---

162   If we follow the Queen's account of the reversal of events in the finger pricking saga, the finger has not been injured at all, so Alice's comment is irrelevant.

163   The sudden transformation into a sheep is one of the magical changes that occasionally occur in Looking-Glass world, unlike Wonderland.

"You may look in front of you, and on both sides, if you like," said the Sheep; "but you ca'n't look *all* around you—unless you've got eyes at the back of your head."[164]

But these, as it happened, Alice had *not* got:[165] so she contented herself with turning round, looking at the shelves as she came to them.

The shop seemed to be full of all manner of curious things—but the oddest part of it all was that, whenever she looked hard at any shelf, to make out exactly what it had on

164   The Sheep is playing with words—Alice did not say she had to see all around herself at the same time.

165   *Alice had NOT got*—a gently ironic remark by our author.

it, that particular shelf was always quite empty, though the others round it were crowded as full as they could hold.

"Things flow about so here!" she said at last in a plaintive tone, after she had spent a minute or so in vainly pursuing a large bright thing, that looked sometimes like a doll and sometimes like a work-box, and was always in the shelf next above the one she was looking at. "And this one is the most provoking of all—but I'll tell you what——" she added, as a sudden thought struck her. "I'll follow it up to the very top shelf of all. It'll puzzle it to go through the ceiling, I expect!"

But even this plan failed: the "thing" went through the ceiling as quietly as possible, as if it were quite used to it.

"Are you a child or a teetotum?" the Sheep said, as she took up another pair of needles. "You'll make me giddy soon, if you go on turning round like that." She was now working with fourteen pairs at once, and Alice couldn't help looking at her in great astonishment.

"How *can* she knit with so many?" the puzzled child thought to herself. "She gets more and more like a porcupine every minute!"

"Can you row?" the Sheep asked, handing her a pair of knitting-needles as she spoke.

"Yes, a little—but not on land—and not with needles——" Alice was beginning to say, when suddenly the needles turned into oars in her hands, and she found they were in a little boat, gliding along between banks:[166] so there was nothing for it but to do her best.

"Feather!" cried the Sheep, as she took up another pair of needles.

This didn't sound like a remark that needed any answer: so Alice said nothing, but pulled away. There was something very queer about the water, she thought, as every now and

166 Another magical transformation.

then the oars got fast in it, and would hardly come out again.[167]

"Feather! Feather!" the Sheep cried again, taking more needles. "You'll be catching a crab directly."[168]

"A dear little crab!" thought Alice, "I should like that."

---

167 Our author is siding totally with Alice—*we* know that the sensation of oars getting apparently stuck in the water is simply a result of not rowing correctly—as does the Sheep.

168 The Sheep is again using a technical rowing term, and again Alice does not understand.

"Didn't you hear me say 'Feather'?" the Sheep cried angrily, taking up quite a bunch of needles.[169]

"Indeed I did," said Alice: "you've said it very often[170]— and very loud. Please where *are* the crabs?"

"In the water, of course!" said the Sheep, sticking some of the needles into her hair, as her hands were full. "Feather, I say!"

"*Why* do you say 'Feather' so often?" Alice asked at last, rather vexed. "I'm not a bird!"

"You are," said the Sheep: "you're a little goose."[171]

This offended Alice a little, so there was no more conversation for a minute or two, while the boat glided gently on, sometimes among the beds of weeds (which made the oars stick fast in the water, worse than ever), and sometimes under trees, but always with the same tall river-banks frowning over their heads.

"Oh, please! There are some scented rushes!" Alice cried in a sudden transport of delight. "There really are—and *such* beauties!"

"You needn't say 'please' to *me* about 'em," the Sheep said, without looking up from her knitting: "I didn't put 'em there, and I'm not going to take 'em away."

"No, but I meant—please, may we wait and pick some?" Alice pleaded. "If you don't mind stopping the boat for a minute."

"How am *I* to stop it?" said the Sheep. "If you leave off rowing, it'll stop of itself."[172]

---

169   It is interesting to note that virtually every time the Sheep speaks throughout this section of the book, a reference is made about her knitting—usually to remark on her taking up more needles.

170   *you've said it very often*—in fact she has only said it three times.

171   *you're a little goose*—one of the very few occasions in the *Alice* books, where a character is actually very rude to Alice.

172   Alice assumes that the Sheep is in general charge of the situation, and as a polite little Victorian child, she thinks it only correct to ask permission to

So the boat was left to drift down the stream as it would, till it glided gently in among the waving rushes. And then the little sleeves were carefully rolled up, and the little arms were plunged in elbow-deep, to get hold of the rushes a good long way down before breaking them off—and for a while Alice forgot all about the Sheep and the knitting, as she bent over the side of the boat, with just the ends of her tangled hair dipping into the water—while with bright eager eyes she caught at one bunch after another of the darling scented rushes.[173]

"I only hope the boat wo'n't tipple over!" she said to herself. "Oh, *what* a lovely one! Only I couldn't quite reach it." And it certainly *did* seem a little provoking ("almost as if it happened on purpose," she thought) that, though she managed to pick plenty of beautiful rushes as the boat glided by, there was always a more lovely one that she couldn't reach.

"The prettiest are always further!" she said at last, with a sigh at the obstinacy of the rushes in growing so far off, as, with flushed cheeks and dripping hair and hands, she scrambled back into her place, and began to arrange her new-found treasures.

What mattered it to her just then that the rushes had begun to fade, and to lose all their scent and beauty, from the very moment that she picked them? Even real scented rushes, you know, last only a very little while[174]—and these, being dream-rushes, melted away almost like snow, as they lay in heaps at her feet—but Alice hardly noticed this, there so many other curious things to think about.

stop.

173   This is a quite lyrical paragraph, where the author becomes totally consumed with Alice's activities, sympathizing with her views on "darling" scented rushes.

174   The third (of five) occasions where the author addresses the reader directly.

They hadn't gone much further before the blade of one of the oars got fast in the water and *wouldn't* come out again (so Alice explained it afterwards), and the consequence was that the handle of it caught her under the chin, and, in spite of a series of little shrieks of "Oh, oh, oh!" from poor Alice, it swept her straight off the seat, and down among the heap of rushes.

However, she wasn't a bit hurt, and was soon up again: the Sheep went on with her knitting all the while, just as if nothing had happened. "That was a nice crab you caught!"[175] she remarked, as Alice got back into her place, very much relieved to find herself still in the boat.

"Was it? I didn't see it," said Alice, peeping cautiously over the side of the boat into the dark water. "I wish it hadn't let go—I should so like a little crab to take home with me!"[176] But the Sheep only laughed scornfully, and went on with her knitting.

"Are there many crabs here?" said Alice.

"Crabs, and all sorts of things," said the Sheep: "plenty of choice, only make up your mind. Now, what *do* you want to buy?"[177]

"To buy!" Alice echoed in a tone that was half astonished and half frightened—for the oars, and the boat, and the river, had vanished all in a moment, and she was back again in the little dark shop.

175   *That was a nice crab you caught*—the Sheep is a little over-critical—the reason the oar got stuck was not in catching a crab (in the rowing sense) but in getting stuck in the weeds.

176   *to take home with me*—Alice is viewing the whole adventure as a type of holiday that will come to an end with her return home.

177   The Sheep realizes, before Alice does, that they are back in the shop (in a third magical transformation)—even so it is odd that the Sheep seems to be suggesting that crabs might be for sale in the shop, which is hardly likely. (Curiously, now the Sheep is back in the shop, there is no further mention of needles or knitting.)

"I should like to buy an egg, please," she said timidly. "How do you sell them?"

"Fivepence farthing for one—twopence for two," the Sheep replied.

"Then two are cheaper than one?" Alice said in a surprised tone, taking out her purse.

"Only you *must* eat them both, if you buy two," said the Sheep.[178]

"Then I'll have *one*, please," said Alice, as she put the money down on the counter. For she thought to herself "They mightn't be at all nice, you know."

The Sheep took the money, and put it away in a box: then she said "I never put things into people's hands—that would never do—you must get it yourself." And so saying, she went off to the other end of the shop, and set the egg upright on a shelf.[179]

"I wonder *why* it wouldn't do?" thought Alice, as she groped her way among the tables and chairs, for the shop was very dark towards the end. "The egg seems to get further away the more I walk towards it. Let me see, is this a chair? Why, it's got branches, I declare! How very odd to find trees growing here! And actually here's a little brook! Well, this is the very queerest shop I ever saw!"

*　　*　　*　　*　　*　　*

　*　　*　　*　　*　　*

*　　*　　*　　*　　*　　*

178　It is unlikely that eggs would be eaten on the shop premises, so the owner would never know whether they were in fact eaten.

179　*The Annotated Alice* makes the point that it is very difficult to place an egg upright. We are not told how the Sheep manages it.

So, she went on, wondering more and more at every step, as everything turned into a tree the moment the moment she came up to it, and she quite expected the egg to do the same.

INTRODUCTION TO CHAPTER VI

*A*gain the preceding chapter ends with Alice alone. She wonders about the egg—which we know is the prelude to one of the most intriguing encounters that Alice faces in the story.

Humpty Dumpty

*H*owever, the egg only got larger and larger, and more and more human:[180] when she had come within a few yards of it, she saw that it had eyes and a nose and mouth; and, when she had come close to it, she saw clearly that it was HUMPTY DUMPTY himself. "It ca'n't be anybody else!" she said to herself. "I'm as certain of it, as if his name were written all over his face!"

It might have been written a hundred times, easily, on that enormous face. Humpty Dumpty was sitting, with his legs crossed like a Turk, on the top of a high wall—such a narrow one that Alice quite wondered how he could keep his balance—and, as his eyes were steadily fixed in the opposite direction, and he didn't take the least notice of her, she thought he must be a stuffed figure, after all.

---

180 *More and more human*—whether Humpty can be described as "human" is
    a debatable point.

"And how exactly like an egg he is!" she said aloud, standing with her hands ready to catch him, for she was every moment expecting him to fall.

"It's *very* provoking," Humpty Dumpty said after a long silence, looking away from Alice[181] as he spoke, "to be called an egg—*very!*"

"I said you *looked* like an egg, Sir," Alice gently explained. "And some eggs are very pretty, you know," she added, hoping to turn her remark into a sort of compliment.

"Some people," said Humpty Dumpty, looking away from her as usual, "have no more sense than a baby!"

Alice didn't know what to say to this: it wasn't at all like conversation, she thought, as he never said anything to *her*; in fact, his last remark was evidently addressed to a tree—so she stood and softly repeated to herself:—

"Humpty Dumpty sat on a wall:
Humpty Dumpty had a great fall.
All the King's horses and all the King's men
Couldn't put Humpty Dumpty in his place again."

"That last line is much too long for the poetry," she added, almost out loud, forgetting that Humpty Dumpty would hear her.[182]

"Don't stand chattering to yourself like that," Humpty Dumpty said, looking at her for the first time, "but tell me your name and your business."

---

181 *looking away from Alice*—we have just been told that his eyes were fixed in the opposite direction—so is this 'looking away' simply part of the already stated direction of his gaze?

182 Some versions of the rhyme have the last line:—'Couldn't put Humpty together again'—which is *not* 'too long for the poetry'. But it is interesting to note that Lewis Carroll always refers to him as 'Humpty Dumpty', never just as 'Humpty'.

"My *name* is Alice, but——"

"It's a stupid name enough!" Humpty Dumpty interrupted impatiently. "What does it mean?"

"*Must* a name mean something?" Alice asked doubtfully.

"Of course it must," Humpty Dumpty said with a short laugh: "*my* name means the shape I am—and a good handsome shape it is, too. With a name like yours, you might be any shape, almost."[183]

"Why do you sit out here all alone?" said Alice, not wishing to begin an argument.

"Why, because there's nobody with me!" cried Humpty Dumpty. "Did you think I didn't know the answer to *that*? Ask another."[184]

"Don't you think you'd be safer down on the ground?" Alice went on, not with any idea of making another riddle, but simply in her good-natured anxiety for the queer creature. "That wall is so *very* narrow!"

"What tremendously easy riddles you ask!" Humpty Dumpty growled out. "Of course I don't think so! Why, if ever I *did* fall off—which there's no chance of—but *if* I did——" Here he pursed up his lips, and looked so solemn and grand that Alice could hardly help laughing. "*If* I *did* fall," he went on, "*the King*[185] *has promised me*—ah, you

183 Humpty Dumpty, when he says a name must mean something, is implying that the only meaning possible is one referring to a person's shape. He is proud of his shape, which makes one wonder why he should have been offended at Alice's earlier comment on his being shaped like an egg, which is surely incontrovertible.

184 Humpty Dumpty is assuming that Alice's question is the first of a string of riddles. Why he should assume this is difficult to fathom, as her question does not sound at all like a riddle. In fact Alice is really asking about the loneliness, not the simple fact of his being on his own.

185 Humpty Dumpty does not specify which King he is referring to, though we later find that it is the White King. This is slightly odd, as the 'Dramatis Personae' at the beginning of the book (in all editions except the final

may turn pale, if you like! You didn't think I was going to say that, did you? *The King has promised me—with his very own mouth—to—to——*"[186]

"To send all his horses and all his men," Alice interrupted, rather unwisely.

"Now I declare that's too bad!" Humpty Dumpty cried, breaking into a sudden passion. "You've been listening at doors—and behind trees—and down chimneys—or you couldn't have known it!"

"I haven't indeed!" Alice said very gently. "It's in a book."

"Ah, well! They may write such things in a *book*," Humpty Dumpty said in a calmer tone. "That's what you call a History of England,[187] that is, Now, take a good look at me!

---

revision of 1897) lists Humpty Dumpty as a "red piece". But perhaps in Looking-Glass land divisions into red and white personae is not too chauvinistic—it is after all "only a game".

186   One wonders why "to—to" is not also in italics.

187   *History of England*—is Humpty Dumpty suggesting that he is a resident of England, rather than "Looking-Glass" land?

I'm one that has spoken to a King, *I* am: mayhap[188] you'll never see such another: and, to show you I'm not proud, you may shake hands with me!" And he grinned almost from ear to ear, as he leant forwards (and as nearly as possible fell off the wall in doing so) and offered Alice his hand. She watched him a little anxiously as she took it. "If he smiled much more the ends of his mouth might meet behind," she thought: "and then I don't know *what* would happen to his head! I'm afraid it would come off!"

"Yes, all his horses and all his men," Humpty Dumpty went on. "They'd pick me up again in a minute, *they* would! However, this conversation is going on a little too fast: let's go back to the last remark but one."

"I'm afraid I ca'n't quite remember it," Alice said, very politely.[189]

"In that case we start afresh," said Humpty Dumpty, "and it's my turn to choose a subject——" ("He talks about it just as if was a game!" thought Alice.) "So here's a question for you. How old did you say you were?"

Alice made a short calculation, and said "Seven years and six months."[190]

---

188 *mayhap*—I wondered if this was one of Lewis Carroll's portmanteau words: a combination of "maybe" and "perhaps"? But Michael Everson informs me that the Oxford English Dictionary gives the earliest date for *maybe* as c. 1400, for *perhaps* as c. 1520, and for *mayhap* as 1533. Nineteenth-century authors Walter Scott, Charles Dickens, and William Morris used it.

189 In fact this is quite a difficult thing to decide. All the "last remarks" have been to do with the possible rescue of Humpty Dumpty in case of a fall. The last remark not related to this scenario would be Alice saying "It's in a book."

190 When she told the White Queen (in Chapter V) that she was "seven and a half, exactly", she had not needed to make any calculation. It is interesting that she phrases her answer differently on the two occasions.

"Wrong!" Humpty Dumpty exclaimed triumphantly. "You never said a word like it!"

"I thought you meant 'How old *are* you?'" Alice explained.

"If I'd meant that, I'd have said it," said Humpty Dumpty.[191]

Alice didn't want to begin another argument, so she said nothing.

"Seven years and six months!" Humpty Dumpty repeated thoughtfully. "An uncomfortable sort of age.[192] Now if you'd asked *my* advice, I'd have said 'Leave off at seven'——but it's too late now."

"I never ask advice about growing," Alice said indignantly.[193]

"Too proud?" the other inquired.

Alice felt even more indignant at this suggestion. "I mean," she said, "that one ca'n't help growing older."[194]

"*One* ca'n't, perhaps," said Humpty Dumpty; "but *two* can. With proper assistance, you might have left off at seven."[195]

"What a beautiful belt you've got on!" Alice suddenly remarked. (They had had quite enough of the subject of age, she thought: and, if they really were to take turns in choosing subjects, it was *her* turn now.) "At least," she corrected herself on second thoughts, "a beautiful cravat, I should have said—no, a belt, I mean—I beg your pardon!"[196] she added in dismay, for Humpty Dumpty looked thoroughly offended,

191 Humpty Dumpty is of course still in "riddle-mode".

192 *An uncomfortable sort of age*—Humpty Dumpty offers no reason for it being an "uncomfortable age". And his advice is somewhat disconcerting.

193 A strange reply—suggesting that the possibility of doing something about growing is a plausible option.

194 Alice explains her previous strange answer.

195 This alarming statement is fully discussed in *The Annotated Alice*.

196 *I beg your pardon*—when Alice uses this phrase a little later, Humpty Dumpty picks up on it immediately. Here, in his anger, he hardly notices it—he is far more concerned with her confusion.

and she began to wish she hadn't chosen that subject. "If only I knew," she thought to herself, "which was neck and which was waist!"

Evidently Humpty Dumpty was very angry, though he said nothing for a minute or two. When he *did* speak again, it was in a deep growl.

"It is a—*most*—*provoking*—thing," he said at last, "when a person doesn't know a cravat from a belt!"

"I know it's very ignorant of me," Alice said, in so humble a tone that Humpty Dumpty relented.

"It's a cravat, child, and a beautiful one, as you say. It's a present from the White King[197] and Queen. There now!"

"Is it really?" said Alice, quite pleased to find that she *had* chosen a good subject, after all.

"They gave it me," Humpty Dumpty continued thoughtfully, as he crossed one knee over the other and clasped his hands round it, "they gave it me—for an un-birthday present."

"I beg your pardon?" Alice said with a puzzled air.[198]

"I'm not offended," said Humpty Dumpty.[199]

"I mean, what *is* an un-birthday present?"

"A present given when it isn't your birthday, of course."

Alice considered a little. "I like birthday presents, best," she said at last.

197 *White King*—Humpty Dumpty, unlike previously, does now specify which King.

198 Lewis Carroll makes great play of the use of the phrase 'I beg your pardon" in *Looking-Glass* (less so in *Wonderland*, where it is used extensively, but usually as an apology for possibly having caused offence, and is not otherwise commented on). In *Looking-Glass*, it usually denotes an apology for possibly not having heard, or understood, the other speaker correctly. When Alice uses the phrase when talking to the White King (see Chapter VII) she evokes a quite different response.

199 *not offended*—in contrast with Alice's earlier "faux pas" when he *was* deeply offended.

"You don't know what you're talking about!" cried Humpty Dumpty.[200] "How many days are there in a year?"

"Three hundred and sixty-five," said Alice.

"And now many birthdays have you?"

"One."

"And if you take one from three hundred and sixty-five, what remains?"

"Three hundred and sixty-four, of course."

Humpty Dumpty looked doubtful. "I'd rather see that done on paper," he said.

Alice couldn't help smiling as she took out her memorandum-book,[201] and worked the sum for him:

$$\begin{array}{r} 365 \\ \underline{1} \\ 364 \end{array}$$

Humpty Dumpty took the book, and looked at it carefully. "That seems to be done right——" he began.

"You're holding it upside down!" Alice interrupted.

"To be sure I was!" Humpty Dumpty said gaily, as she turned it round for him. "I thought it looked a little queer. As I was saying, that *seems* to be done right—though I haven't time to look it over thoroughly just now—and that shows that there are three hundred and sixty-four days when you might get un-birthday presents——"

"Certainly," said Alice.

200   Humpty Dumpty takes a rather mercenary view of presents, Alice on the other hand sees presents as being an integral part of birthday celebrations, and therefore to be preferred.

201   *memorandum book*—this is the first time we learn that Alice has such an item in her pocket (as well as a pencil, and purse with money)—In Chapter I we learnt that the White King also carried one in his pocket.

And only *one* for birthday presents, you know. There's glory for you!"

"I don't know what you mean by 'glory,'" Alice said.

Humpty Dumpty smiled contemptuously. "Of course you don't—till I tell you. I meant 'there's a nice knock-down argument for you!'"

"But 'glory' doesn't mean 'a nice knock-down argument,'" Alice objected.

"When *I* use a word," Humpty Dumpty said, in rather a scornful tone, "it means just what I choose it to mean—neither more nor less."

"The question is," said Alice, "whether you *can* make words mean so many different things."

"The question is," said Humpty Dumpty, "which is to be master——that's all."

Alice was too much puzzled to say anything; so after a minute Humpty Dumpty began again. "They've a temper, some of them—particularly verbs: they're the proudest—adjectives you can do anything with, but not verbs—however, *I* can manage the whole lot of them! Impenetrability! That's what *I* say!"

"Would you tell me, please," said Alice, "what that means?"

"Now you talk like a sensible child," said Humpty Dumpty, looking very much pleased. "I meant by 'impenetrability' that we've had enough of that subject, and it would be just as well if you'd mention what you mean to do next, as I suppose you don't mean to stop here all the rest of your life."

"That's a great deal to make one word mean," Alice said in a thoughtful tone.[202]

"When I make a word do a lot of work like that," said Humpty Dumpty, "I always pay it extra."

---

202   The conversation is diverted from Alice replying to the lengthy meaning of "impenetrability" to a discussion on the advisability of using language in this way.

"Oh!" said Alice. She was too much puzzled[203] to make any other remark.

"Ah, you should see 'em come round me of a Saturday night,"[204] Humpty Dumpty went on, wagging his head gravely from side to side, "for to get their wages, you know."

(Alice didn't venture to ask what he paid them with; and so you see I ca'n't tell *you*.)[205]

"You seem very clever at explaining words, Sir,"[206] said Alice. "Would you kindly tell me the meaning of the poem called '*Jabberwocky*'?"

"Let's hear it," said Humpty Dumpty. "I can explain all the poems that ever were invented—and a good many that haven't been invented just yet."[207]

This sounded very hopeful, so Alice repeated the first verse:—

> *"'Twas brillig, and the slithy toves*
> *Did gyre and gimble in the wabe:*
> *All mimsy were the borogoves,*
> *And the mome raths outgrabe."*

---

203 *too much puzzled*—the second time in this short conversation that this phrase has been used.

204 *Saturday night*—presumably it was the custom in Victorian times in England to give wages out on a Saturday night. In 20th- and 21st-century England, Friday night is the norm.

205 *ca'n't tell you*—the fourth (of five) instances where the author addresses the reader directly.

206 This is the second time Alice has addressed Humpty Dumpty as "Sir"—the only character thus addressed in *Looking-Glass*. It is here used to underline the fact that Alice is now behaving as pupil towards school teacher.

207 It is interesting that Humpty Dumpty views the writing of poetry as a matter of invention.

"That's enough to begin with," Humpty Dumpty interrupted: "there are plenty of hard words there.[208] '*Brillig*'[209] means four o'clock in the afternoon—the time when begin *broiling* things for dinner."

"That'll do very well," said Alice: "and '*slithy*'?"

---

208   *plenty of hard words there*—how true. In fact every word is "hard" apart from the linking words—'Twas; and the; Did; and; in the; all; were the; and the".

209   *brillig*—A fairly restrictive meaning, one might suggest—not every evening meal involves broiling items.

"Well, *'slithy'* means 'lithe and slimy.' 'Lithe' is the same as 'active.'[210] You see it's like a portmanteau—there are two meaning packed up into one word."

"I see it now," Alice remarked thoughtfully: "and what are *'toves'*?"

"Well, *'toves'* are something like badgers—they're something like lizards—and they're something like corkscrews."

"They must be very curious-looking creatures."

"They are that," said Humpty Dumpty: "also they make their nests[211] under sun-dials—also they live on cheese."

"And what's to *'gyre'* and to *'gimble'*?"

"To *'gyre'* is to go round and round like a gyroscope. To *'gimble'* is to make holes like a gimblet."[212]

"And *'the wabe'* is the grass-plot round a sun-dial, I suppose?" said Alice, surprised as her own ingenuity.

"Of course it is. It's called *'wabe,'* you know, because it goes a long way before it, and a long way behind it——"

"And a long way beyond it on either side," Alice added.[213]

"Exactly so. Well then, *'mimsy'* is 'flimsy and miserable' (there's another portmanteau for you). And a *'borogove'* is a thin shabby-looking bird with its feathers sticking out all round—something like a live mop."

"And then *'mome raths'*?" said Alice. "I'm afraid I'm giving you a great deal of trouble."

---

210 It is interesting that Humpty Dumpty also defines "lithe" (a "normal" word) for Alice. He is assuming it to be a word that she would not be familiar with.

211 One might think it strange that a creature the size of a badger should make nests. (Michael Everson reminds me that gorillas make them.)

212 *gimble*—if we follow Humpty Dumpty's talking of portmanteau words, it would seem more likely that "gimble" is a portmanteau word from "gambol" and "nimbly". In addition, Carroll's spelling of "gimblet" is curious—the usual spelling is "gimlet". (Michael Everson points out that the Middle English word was borrowed from Old French *guimbelet*.)

213 All this suggests that the grass-plot is huge.

"Well, a *'rath'* is a sort of green pig: but *'mome'* I'm not certain about.[214] I think it's short for 'from home'—meaning they'd lost their way, you know."

"And what does *'outgrabe'* mean?"

"Well, *'outgribing'* is something between bellowing and whistling, with a kind of sneeze in the middle: however, you'll hear it done, maybe—down in the wood yonder[215]—and, when you've once heard it, you'll be *quite* content. Who's been repeating all that hard stuff to you?"[216]

"I read it in a book," said Alice. "But I *had* some poetry repeated to me much easier than that, by—Tweedledee, I think it was."[217]

"As to poetry, you know," said Humpty Dumpty, stretching out one of his great hands, "*I* can repeat poetry as well as other folk, if it comes to that——"

"Oh, it needn't come to that!" Alice hastily said, hoping to keep him from beginning.[218]

214 *not certain about*—the first time Humpty Dumpty has been unsure of his definitions—rather be-lying his statement earlier that he "can explain all the poems that ever were invented".

215 *"you'll hear it done, maybe—down in the wood yonder"*—Humpty Dumpty does not explain this—is he suggesting that mome raths are down in the wood?

216 Alice does not recite the rest of "Jabberwocky", so we never hear Humpty Dumpty's explanations for the other "hard words"—*Jubjub, frumious, Bandersnatch, vorpal, manxome, Tumtum, uffish, whiffling, tulgey, burbled, galumphing, beamish, frabjous, Callooh, Callay, chortled*. Lewis Carroll explains "frumious" in the Preface to *The Hunting of the Snark*. For suggestions for the meaning of the other words—see *The Annotated Alice*—where we learn that "whiffling" is not a Carrollian word. Even so, one might suggest in the Carroll context, it could be a portmanteau word from "whistle" and "sniff" (or "sniffle"); similarly *"tulgey"* could be a portmanteau word from "turgid" and "ugly".

217 It was.

218 A forlorn hope, judging by Alice's experience throughout the book.

"The piece I'm going to repeat," he went on without noticing his remark, "was written entirely for your amusement."[219]

Alice felt that in that case she really *ought* to listen to it; so she sat down,[220] and said "Thank you" rather sadly.

> *"In winter, when the fields are white,*
> *I sing this song for your delight——*

only I don't sing it," he added, as an explanation.

"I see you don't," said Alice.

"If you can *see* whether I'm singing or not, you've sharper eyes than most," Humpty Dumpty remarked severely. Alice was silent.

> *"In spring, when woods are getting green,*
> *I'll try and tell you what I mean:"*

"Thank you very much," said Alice

> *"In summer, when the days are long*
> *Perhaps you'll understand the song:*
>
> *In autumn, when the leaves are brown,*
> *Take pen and ink, and write it down."*

"I will, if I can remember it so long," said Alice.

"You needn't go on making remarks like that," Humpty Dumpty said: "they're not sensible, and they put me out."[221]

---

219 This suggests almost prophetic insight, seeing that they have only just met—for the first time.

220 *sat down*—one wonders what she sat on—there has been no mention of anything suitable.

221 Humpty Dumpty is being a little unfair. Alice's remarks are eminently sensible, and a genuine response to what has been said. It is interesting

"I sent a message to the fish:
I told them 'This is what I wish.'

The little fishes of the sea,
They sent an answer back to me.

The little fishes' answer was
"We cannot do it, Sir, because——"'

"I'm afraid I don't quite understand," said Alice.[222]

"It gets easier further on," Humpty Dumpty replied.

"I sent to them again to say
'It will be better to obey.'

The fishes answered, with a grin,
'Why, what a temper you are in!'

I told them once, I told them twice:
They would not listen to advice.

I took a kettle large and new,
Fit for the deed I had to do.

My heart went hop, my heart went thump:
I filled the kettle at the pump.

---

that this is the only poem in the book which is interrupted either by the narrator—or Alice (apart from a brief interruption at the beginning of *The Walrus and the Carpenter*).

222 An eminently reasonable comment—one assumes that the fish were about to say they could not do it, because no details of the request had been given, but we are destined not to be told either.

Then some one came to me and said
'The little fishes are in bed.'[223]

I said to him, I said it plain,
'Then you must wake them up again.'

I said it very loud and clear,
I went and shouted in his ear."

Humpty Dumpty raised his voice almost to a scream as he repeated this verse, and Alice thought, with a shudder, "I wouldn't have been the messenger for *anything!*"

223   *in bed*—a curious statement; quite how fish can go to bed is never explained.

"But he was very stiff and proud:
He said 'You needn't shout so loud!'

And he was very proud and stiff:
He said 'I'd go and wake them, if——'

I took a corkscrew from the shelf:
I went to wake them up myself.

And when I found the door was locked,[224]
I pulled and pushed and kicked and knocked.

And when I found the door was shut,
I tried to turn the handle, but——"[225]

There was a long pause.

"Is that all? Alice timidly asked.

"That's all," said Humpty Dumpty. "Good-bye."

This was rather sudden, Alice thought: but, after such a *very* strong hint that she ought to be going, she felt that it would hardly be civil to stay. So she got up, and held out her hand. "Good-bye, till we meet again!" she said as cheerfully as she could.

---

224 *door was locked*—further evidence of the anthropomorphism of the fish. And one would expect Humpty Dumpty to mention that the door was shut, before noting that it was also locked—though this would of course spoil the dénouement of the poem.

225 It is strange, knowing of Humpty Dumpty's fondness for words, that this poem consists almost entirely of monosyllabic words—possibly an intentional ironic joke by our author? *The Annotated Alice* quotes Richard Kelly (*Lewis Carroll*: Twayne 1977) that the poem "has to be the worst poem in the *Alice* books"—a sentiment that is hard to argue with.

"I shouldn't know you again if we *did* meet," Humpty Dumpty replied in a discontented tone, giving her one of his fingers to shake: "you're so exactly like other people."

"The face is what one goes by, generally," Alice remarked in a thoughtful tone.

"That's just what I complain of," said Humpty Dumpty. "Your face is the same as everybody has—the two eyes, so——" (marking their places in the air with his thumb) "nose in the middle, mouth under. It's always the same. Now if you had the two eyes on the same side of the nose, for instance—or the mouth at the top—that would be *some* help."

"It wouldn't look nice," Alice objected. But Humpty Dumpty only shut his eyes, and said "Wait till you've tried."[226]

Alice waited a minute to see if he would speak again, but, as he never opened his eyes or took any further notice of her, she said "Good-bye!" once more, and, getting no answer to this, she quietly walked away: but she couldn't help saying to herself, as she went, "Of all the unsatisfactory——" (she repeated this aloud, as it was a great comfort to have such a long word to say) "of all the unsatisfactory people I *ever* met——" she never finished the sentence, for at this moment a heavy crash[227] shook the forest from end to end.

---

226 An impossible suggestion of course, but reminiscent of his earlier suggestion that she could have left off growing at seven.

227 Although not stated, we can only assume that the crash is Humpty Dumpty having his "great fall".

INTRODUCTION TO CHAPTER VII

*O*nce more the preceding chapter ends with Alice alone. Curiously, Humpty Dumpty's problems are totally ignored in the coming chapter, as we engage in one of the few "crowd" scenes in the book, meeting a whole host of new characters, some oddly reminiscent of certain characters from *Wonderland*.

The Lion
and the Unicorn

*T*he next moment soldiers came running through the wood, at first in twos and threes, then ten or twenty together, and at last in such crowds that they seemed to fill the whole forest. Alice got behind a tree, for fear of being run over, and watched them go by.

She thought that in all her life she had never seen soldiers so uncertain on their feet: they were always tripping over something or other, and whenever one went down, several more always fell over him, so that the ground was soon covered with little heaps of men.[228]

Then came the horses. Having four feet, these managed rather better than the foot-soldiers; but even *they* stumbled now and then; and it seemed to be a regular rule that, whenever a horse stumbled, the rider fell off instantly. The

---

228　The soldiers all falling over could be an ironic reference to their intended role in picking up Humpty Dumpty after *his* fall.

confusion got worse every moment, and Alice was very glad to get out of the wood and into an open place, where she found the White King seated on the ground, busily writing in his memorandum-book.[229]

---

229 We are already aware of the King's memorandum book—from several references to it in Chapter I.

"I've sent them all!" the King cried in a tone of delight, on seeing Alice. "Did you happen to meet any soldiers, my dear,[230] as you came through the wood?"

"Yes, I did," said Alice: "several thousand, I should think."

"Four thousand two hundred and seven, that's the exact number," the King said, referring to his book. "I couldn't send all the horses, you know, because two of them are wanted in the game. And I haven't sent the two Messengers, either.[231] They're both gone to the town.[232] Just look along the road, and tell me if you can see either of them."

"I see nobody on the road," said Alice.

"I only wish *I* had such eyes,"[233] the King remarked in a fretful tone. "To be able to see Nobody![234] And at that distance too! Why, it's as much as *I* can do to see real people, by this light!"

All this was lost on Alice, who was still looking intently along the road, shading her eyes with one hand, "I see somebody now!" she exclaimed at last. "But he's coming very slowly—and what curious attitudes he goes into!" (For the Messenger kept skipping up and down, and wriggling like an eel, as he came along, with his great hands spread out like fans on each side.)

230 *my dear*—a phrase used a lot by the King—particularly towards the White Queen in Chapter I. Alice is only addressed this way by the Gentleman in White Paper in Chapter III, and the King here.

231 The King is more interested in the accuracy of his numbers than in the purpose of them being sent at all—in fact we hear no more either of the soldiers, the horses, or their success, or not, in carrying out any rescue of Humpty Dumpty.

232 *They're both gone to the town*—slightly oddly phrased—would it not be better to say "They've both gone to the town"?

233 *I only wish I had such eyes*—an interesting remark in view of the very recent discussion on eyes with Humpty Dumpty.

234 *nobody/Nobody*—a typical Carroll touch, as the word suddenly takes on anthropomorphic status.

"Not at all," said the King. "He's an Anglo-Saxon Messenger—and those are Anglo-Saxon attitudes. He only does them when he's happy. His name is Haigha." (He pronounced it so as to rhyme with "mayor.")

"I love my love with an H,"[235] Alice couldn't help beginning, "because he is Happy. I hate him with an H, because he is Hideous. I fed him[236] with—with—Ham-sandwiches and Hay. His name is Haigha, and he lives——"

"He lives on the Hill,"[237] the King remarked simply, without the least idea that he was joining in the game, while Alice was still hesitating for the name of a town beginning with H. "The other Messenger's called Hatta. I must have *two*, you know—to come and go. One to come, and one to go."

"I beg your pardon?" said Alice.

"It isn't respectable to beg," said the King.[238]

"I only meant that I didn't understand," said Alice. "Why one to come and one to go?"

"Don't I tell you?" the King repeated impatiently. "I must have *two*—to fetch and carry. One to fetch, and one to carry."

At this moment the Messenger arrived: he was far too much out of breath to say a word, and could only wave his hands about, and make the most fearful faces at the poor King.

"This young lady[239] loves you with an H," the King said, introducing Alice in the hope of turning off the Messenger's

---

235   *I love my love with an H*—Alice starts the game because she has been reminded of it by the coincidence of "Haigha" alliterating with "happy" and the structure of the King's sentence.

236   *fed him*—to be consistent with tenses, "fed" really should be "feed".

237   Although our author says the King has no idea he is joining in the game, he still says *Hill* (which the author has spelt with an uppercase H).

238   A different response to Alice's use of "I beg your pardon" from Humpty Dumpty's in Chapter VI.

239   *young lady*—this, and a little later in the current chapter are the only times in *Looking-Glass* where Alice is referred to as a "young lady"—possibly

attention from himself—but it was of no use—the Anglo-Saxon attitudes only got more extraordinary every moment, while the great eyes rolled wildly from side to side.

"You alarm me!" said the King. "I feel faint——give me a ham sandwich!"[240]

On which the Messenger, to Alice's great amusement, opened a bag that hung round his neck, and handed a sandwich to the King, who devoured it greedily.

"Another sandwich!" said the King.

"There's nothing but hay left now," the Messenger said, peeping into the bag.[241]

here on account of the more adult concept of being in love. (In *Wonderland*, the March Hare invites the "young lady" to tell a story, the Queen urges the Gryphon to take the "young lady" to meet the Mock Turtle, and the Gryphon invites the Mock Turtle to narrate his story to the "young lady".)

240 *ham sandwich*—the second time such a sandwich has been mentioned—this time there is no hyphen.

241 The bag contains ham sandwiches and hay—just as Alice had said when

"Hay, then," the King murmured in a faint whisper.

Alice was glad to see that it revived him a good deal. "There's nothing like eating hay when you're faint," he remarked to her, as he munched away.

"I should think throwing cold water over you would be better," Alice suggested: "—or some sal-volatile."

"I didn't say there was nothing *better*," the King replied. "I said there was nothing *like* it." Which Alice did not venture to deny.

"Who did you pass on the road?" the King went on, holding his hand to the Messenger for some more hay.

"Nobody," said the Messenger.

"Quite right," said the King: "this young lady saw him too. So of course Nobody walks slower[242] than you."

"I do my best," the Messenger said in a sullen tone. "I'm sure nobody[243] walks much faster than I do!"

"He ca'n't do that," said the King. "or else he'd have been here first. However, now you've got your breath, you may tell us what's happening in the town."

"I'll whisper it," said the Messenger, putting his hands to his mouth in the shape of a trumpet and stooping so as to get close to the King's ear. Alice was sorry for this, as she wanted to hear the news too. However, instead of whispering, he simply shouted, at the top of his voice, "They're at it again!"[244]

"Do you call *that* a whisper?" cried the poor King, jumping up and shaking himself. "If you do such a thing again, I'll

playing the H game earlier—a delightful self fulfilling prophecy.

242 *slower*—poor grammar by the King—"more slowly" would be more correct. You might also say that when he said "Who did you pass on the road?" he should have said "Whom", but one must not be too pedantic.

243 Here "nobody" now has a lowercase "n", which adds to the confusion, as the King is still thinking positively about "Nobody".

244 The Messenger's behaviour is reminiscent of Humpty Dumpty shouting in the ear of *his* Messenger.

have you buttered![245] It went through and through my head like an earthquake!"

"It would have to be a very tiny earthquake!" thought Alice. "Who are at it again?" she ventured to ask.

"Why, the Lion and the Unicorn, of course," said the King.[246]

"Fighting for the crown?"

"Yes, to be sure," said the King: "and the best of the joke is, that it's *my* crown all the while! Let's run and see them." And they trotted off, Alice repeating to herself, as she ran, the words of the old song:—

"The Lion and the Unicorn were fighting for the crown:
The Lion beat the Unicorn all round the town.
Some gave them white bread, some gave them brown:
Some gave them plum-cake and drummed them out of town."

"Does——the one——that wins——get the crown?" she asked, as well as she could, for the run was putting her quite out of breath.

"Dear me, no!" said the King. "What an idea!"

"Would you—be good enough——" Alice panted out, after running a little further, "to stop a minute—just to get—one's breath again?"

"I'm *good* enough," the King said, "only I'm not *strong* enough.[247] You see, a minute goes by so fearfully quick.[248] You might just as well try to stop a Bandersnatch!"

---

245   *have you buttered*—a novel punishment—quite what this might entail is not vouchsafed.

246   All thoughts of Humpty Dumpty and his fate are now totally forgotten.

247   *I'm not STRONG enough*—since he has initiated the run, he could of course stop whenever he liked.

248   *so fearfully quick*—another example of the King's poor grammar. He should of course have said *so fearfully quickly*.

Alice had no more breath for talking; so they trotted on in silence, till they came into sight of a great crowd, in the middle of which the Lion and the Unicorn were fighting. They were in such a cloud of dust, that at first Alice could not make out which was which; but she soon managed to distinguish the Unicorn by his horn.

They placed themselves close to where Hatta, the other Messenger, was standing watching the fight, with a cup of tea in one hand and a piece of bread-and-butter in the other.

"He's only just out of prison[249] and he hadn't finished his tea when he was sent in," Haigha whispered to Alice: "and

249 *just out of prison*—we are given no reason why he was in prison. Is this a veiled reference to the Queen of Hearts' anger at the Hatter's poor singing at the concert mentioned at the Mad Tea Party in Wonderland? He was ordered to be executed at that time, but the order was never carried out— possibly the prison sentence was a substitute punishment? But this is all speculation, as the Hatter in Wonderland is only an "alter ego" of Hatta in Looking-Glass land.

they only give them oyster-shells in there—so you see he's very hungry and thirsty. How are you, dear child?"[250] he went on, putting his arm affectionately round Hatta's neck.

Hatta looked round and nodded, and went on with his bread-and-butter.[251]

"Were you happy in prison, dear child?"[252] said Haigha.

Hatta looked round once more, and this time a tear of two trickled down his cheek; but not a word would he say.

"Speak, ca'n't you!" Haigha cried out impatiently. But Hatta only munched away, and drank some more tea.

"Speak, wo'n't you!" cried the King. "How are they getting on with the fight?"

Hatta made a desperate effort, and swallowed a large piece of bread-and-butter. "They're getting on very well," he said in a choking voice: "each of them has been down about eighty-seven times."[253]

"Then I suppose they'll soon bring the white bread and the brown?" Alice ventured to remark.

"It's waiting for 'em now," said Hatta; "this is a bit of it as I'm eating."[254]

---

250 *dear child*—quite why Haigha addresses Hatta in this way, is never explained.

251 The tea and bread-and-butter are of course a reminder to the child reader of the "Mad Tea-Party" in Wonderland.

252 Again, quite why Haigha should address Hatta as "dear child" is never explained.

253 *about eighty-seven times*—a mathematical joke by our author? If using an approximation, the obvious thing would be to round the numbers up (or down)—say to "ninety"—rather than the employ the over-precise "eighty-seven".

254 Hatta speaks in a working-class manner, as befits his "servant status" here, unlike his alter-ego in Wonderland. Although he says "this is a bit of it as I'm eating"—the reference to "bread-and-butter" is, of course, a conscious reference to the bread-and-butter his alter ego was eating at the trial in Wonderland.

There was a pause in the fight just then, and the Lion and the Unicorn sat down, panting, while the King called out "Ten minutes allowed for refreshments!" Haigha and Hatta set to work at once, carrying round trays of white and brown bread. Alice took a piece to taste, but it was *very* dry.[255]

"I don't think they'll fight any more to-day," the King said to Hatta; "go and order the drums to begin." And Hatta went bounding away like a grasshopper.[256]

For a minute or two Alice stood silent, watching him. Suddenly she brightened up. "Look, look!" she cried, pointing eagerly. "There's the White Queen running across the country! She came flying out of the wood over yonder——how fast those Queens *can* run!"

"There's some enemy after her, no doubt," the King said, without even looking round. "That wood's full of them."

"But aren't you going to run and help her?" Alice asked, very much surprised at his taking it so quietly.

"No use, no use!" said the King. "She runs so fearfully quick.[257] You might just as well try to catch a Bandersnatch! But I'll make a memorandum about her, if you like——she's a dear good creature," he repeated softly to himself, as he opened his memorandum-book. "Do you spell 'creature' with a double 'e'?"

At this moment the Unicorn sauntered by them, with his hands in his pockets. "I had the best of it this time?" he said to the King, just glancing at him as he passed.[258]

---

255 It would appear that only Hatta has any butter on his bread.

256 We assume that Hatta, like Haigha, is also an "Anglo-Saxon Messenger," though this is not stated directly. If he is—does he "bound away like a grasshopper," on account of the attendant "Anglo-Saxon attitudes" which might interfere with normal running?

257 *fearfully quick*—another lapse of grammar by the King, and another reference to the problems involved in catching a Bandersnatch—speed is obviously of the essence.

258 The Unicorn's statement is in fact a question, so he is not certain about it.

"A little—a little," the King replied, rather nervously. "You shouldn't have run him through with your horn, you know."[259]

"It didn't hurt him," the Unicorn said carelessly, and he was going on, when his eye happened to fall upon Alice: he turned round instantly, and stood for some time looking at her with an air of the deepest disgust.

"What—is—this?" he said at last.

"This is a child!" Haigha replied eagerly, coming round in front of Alice to introduce her, and spreading out both his hands towards her in an Anglo-Saxon attitude. "We only found it[260] to-day. It's as large as life, and twice as natural!"[261]

"I always thought they were fabulous monsters!" said the Unicorn. "Is it alive?"

"It can talk," said Haigha solemnly.

The Unicorn looked dreamily at Alice, and said "Talk, child."

Alice could not help her lips curling up into a smile as she began: "Do you know, I always thought Unicorns were fabulous monsters, too? I never saw one alive before!"

"Well, now that we *have* seen each other," said the Unicorn, "if you'll believe in me, I'll believe in you. Is that a bargain?"

"Yes, if you like," said Alice.

The King responds to the question.

259   The King's reply implies that there are definite rules to be observed in the fighting.

260   *found it*—in using the word "it", Haigha is responding to the Unicorn's query which used the words "what is this?" which implies an inanimate object. It is rather charming that Haigha should refer to Alice's arrival on the scene, as her being "found".

261   *large as life and twice as natural*—a memorable phrase—invented here by Carroll, and now a sure part of the language.

"Come, fetch out the plum-cake, old man!"[262] the Unicorn went on, turning from her to the King. "None of your brown bread for me!"

"Certainly—certainly!" the King muttered, and beckoned to Haigha. "Open the bag!" he whispered. "Quick! Not that one—that's full of hay!"

Haigha took a large cake out of the bag, and gave it to Alice to hold, while he got out a dish and carving-knife. How they all came out of it Alice couldn't guess. It was just like a conjuring-trick, she thought.

The Lion had joined them while this was going on: he looked very tired and sleepy, and his eyes were half shut. "What's this!" he said, blinking lazily at Alice, and speaking in a deep hollow tone that sounded like the tolling of a great bell.

262   *old man*—the Unicorn does not address the King as "Your Majesty" but in what can only be described as a patronizing manner, implying a rather superior status—the King responds appropriately.

"Ah, what *is* it, now?" the Unicorn cried eagerly. "You'll never guess! *I* couldn't."[263]

The Lion looked at Alice wearily. "Are you animal—or vegetable—or mineral?" he said, yawning at every other word.

"It's a fabulous monster!" the Unicorn cried out, before Alice could reply.

"Then hand round the plum-cake, Monster," the Lion said, lying down and putting his chin on his paws. "And sit down, both of you," (to the King and the Unicorn): "fair play with the cake, you know!"

The King was evidently very uncomfortable at having to sit down between the two great creatures; but there was no other place for him.

"What a fight we might have for the crown, *now!*" the Unicorn said, looking slyly up at the crown,[264] which the poor King was nearly shaking off his head, he trembled so much.

"I should win easy," said the Lion.[265]

"I'm not so sure of that," said the Unicorn.

"Why, I beat you all round the town, you chicken!" the Lion replied angrily, half getting up as he spoke.

Here the King interrupted, to prevent the quarrel going on: he was very nervous, and his voice quite quivered. "All round the town?" he said. "That's a good long way. Did you go by the old bridge, or the market-place? You get the best view by the old bridge."

---

263 The Lion and Unicorn are speaking amicably to each other, which suggests that the earlier fighting was really all just a game.

264 *looking slyly up at the crown*—it has been established that the King is much smaller than the "two great creatures"—so one would have expected the Unicorn to look *down* at the crown.

265 Another lapse of grammar—this time by the Lion—he should have said "easily".

"I'm sure I don't know," the Lion growled out as he lay down again. "There was too much dust to see anything.[266] What a time the Monster is, cutting up the cake!"

Alice had seated herself on the bank of a little brook, with the great dish on her knees, and was sawing away diligently with the knife. "It's very provoking!" she said, in reply to the Lion (she was getting quite used to being called "the Monster"). "I've cut several slices already, but they always join on again!"

"You don't know how to manage Looking-glass cakes," the Unicorn remarked. "Hand it round first, and cut it afterwards."[267]

This sounded nonsense, but Alice very obediently got up, and carried the dish round, and the cake divided itself into three pieces as she did so. "*Now* cut it up," said the Lion, as she returned to her place with the empty dish.[268]

"I say, this isn't fair!" cried the Unicorn, as Alice sat with the knife in her hand, very much puzzled how to begin. "The Monster has given the Lion twice as much as me!"[269]

"She's[270] kept none for herself, anyhow," said the Lion. "Do you like plum-cake, Monster?"

But before Alice could answer him, the drums began.

---

266 *too much dust to see anything*—the Lion doesn't argue that as they were fighting it was hardly the time to admire a view.

267 Another example of our author making a single point about reversal etc. Elsewhere in the book, there is no such problem.

268 The Lion offers the second piece of advice—he and the Unicorn are sharing the instructions.

269 In *The Annotated Alice* it is pointed out that this is the "Lion's share" (as in Aesop's *Fable*).

270 The Lion, unlike the Unicorn and Haigha, delightfully assumes Alice is female—even though she is still, in his eyes, a fabulous monster.

Where the noise came from, she couldn't make out: the air seemed full of it, and it rang through and through her head till she felt quite deafened. She started to her feet, and sprang across the little brook in her terror,

          *   *   *   *   *   *

            *   *   *   *   *

          *   *   *   *   *   *

and had just time to see the Lion and the Unicorn rise to their feet,[271] with angry looks at being interrupted in their

271   *had just time to see the Lion and the Unicorn rise to their feet*—as Alice springs across the brook, it would appear that the previous scenario disappears totally—hence her musing on dreams in the next chapter.

feast,[272] before she dropped to her knees, and put her hands over her ears, vainly trying to shut out the dreadful uproar.

"If *that* doesn't 'drum them out of town,'" she thought to herself, "nothing ever will!"

---

272   *their feast*—whether brown and white bread + plum-cake constitute a "feast" must be open to doubt.

INTRODUCTION TO CHAPTER VIII

*O*nce more the preceding chapter ends with Alice alone. We are now well used to this tradition, and look forward to meetings with more new characters. Some have seen the White Knight as a personification of Lewis Carroll himself, and certainly the meeting is extensive, covering two chapters.

"It's My Own Invention"

After a while the noise seemed gradually to die away, till all was dead silence, and Alice lifted up her head in some alarm. There was no one to be seen, and her first thought was that she must have been dreaming[273] about the Lion and the Unicorn and those queer Anglo-Saxon Messengers. However, there was the great dish still lying at her feet, on which she had tried to cut the plum-cake, "So I wasn't dreaming, after all," she said to herself, "unless— unless we're all part of the same dream. Only I do hope it's *my* dream, and not the Red King's! I don't like belonging to another person's dream," she went on in a rather complaining tone: "I've a great mind to go and wake him, and see what happens!"

---

273   *must have been dreaming*—the whole adventure is of course Alice's dream (as we discover at the end of the book), so her musings on a dream within a dream verge, as it were, on the surreal.

At this moment her thoughts were interrupted by a loud shouting of "Ahoy! Ahoy! Check!" and a Knight, dressed in crimson armour, came galloping down upon her, brandishing a great club. Just as he reached her, the horse stopped suddenly: "You're my prisoner!" the Knight cried, as he tumbled off his horse.

Startled as she was, Alice was more frightened for him than for herself at the moment, and watched him with some anxiety as he mounted again. As soon as he was comfortably in the saddle, he began once more "You're my——" but here another voice broke in "Ahoy! Ahoy! Check!" and Alice looked round in some surprise for the new enemy.

This time it was a White Knight. He drew up at Alice's side, and tumbled off his horse just as the Red Knight had done: then he got on again, and the two Knights sat and looked at each other for some time without speaking. Alice looked from one to the other in some bewilderment.

"She's *my* prisoner, you know!" the Red Knight said at last.

"Yes, but then *I* came and rescued her!" the White Knight replied.

"Well, we must fight for her, then," said the Red Knight, as he took up his helmet (which hung from the saddle, and was something in the shape of a horse's head) and put it on.[274]

"You will observe the Rules of Battle, of course?" the White Knight remarked, putting on his helmet too.

"I always do," said the Red Knight, and they began banging away at each other with such fury that Alice got behind a tree to be out of the way of the blows.

---

274 This is the third battle, or fight in the book (after the Tweedles, and the Lion and Unicorn). Is this a reflection on the Game of Chess being acted out throughout the book? Chess can be viewed as an ongoing adversarial combat.

"I wonder, now, what the Rules of Battle are," she said to herself, as she watched the fight, timidly peeping out from her hiding-place. "One Rule seems to be, that if one Knight hits the other, he knocks him off his horse; and, if he misses, he tumbles off himself—and another Rule seems to be that they hold their clubs with their arms, as if they were Punch and Judy——what a noise they make when they tumble! Just like a whole set of fire-irons falling into the fender! And how quiet the horses are! They let them get on and off them just as if they were tables!"

Another Rule of Battle, that Alice had not noticed,[275] seemed to be that they always fell on their heads; and the battle ended with their both falling off in this way, side by

275 *that Alice had not noticed*—our author is now agreeing with Alice that the Rules can be deduced from observing the battle.

side. When they got up again, they shook hands, and then the Red Knight mounted and galloped off.

"It was a glorious victory,[276] wasn't it?" said the White Knight, as he came up panting.

"I don't know," Alice said doubtfully. "I don't want to be anybody's prisoner. I want to be a Queen."

"So you will, when you've crossed the next brook," said the White Knight. "I'll see you safe to the end of the wood[277]— and then I must go back, you know. That's the end of my move."

"Thank you very much," said Alice. "May I help you off with your helmet?" It was evidently more than he could manage by himself: however she managed to shake him out of it at last.

"Now one can breathe more easily," said the Knight, putting back his shaggy hair with both hands, and turning his gentle face and large mild eyes to Alice. She thought she had never seen such a strange-looking soldier in all her life.

He was dressed in tin armour, which seemed to fit him very badly, and he had a queer-shaped little deal box fastened across his shoulders, upside-down, and with the lid hanging open. Alice looked at it with great curiosity.

"I see you're admiring my little box," the Knight said in a friendly tone. "It's my own invention—to keep clothes and sandwiches in. You see I carry it upside-down, so that the rain ca'n't get in."

"But the things can get *out*," Alice gently remarked. "Do you know the lid's open?"

276 *glorious victory*—the White Knight is using the word glorious in Humpty Dumpty's sense of the word—i.e. "a nice knock-down" victory.

277 *I'll see you safe to the end of the wood*—shows the rather charming side of the White Knight's character; such concern for Alice's progress is not shared by many other characters in the story.

"I didn't know it," the Knight said, a shade of vexation passing over his face. "Then all the things must have fallen out! And the box is no use without them."[278] He unfastened it as he spoke, and was just going to throw it into the bushes, when a sudden thought seemed to strike him, and he hung it carefully on a tree. "Can you guess why I did that?" he said to Alice.

Alice shook her head.

"In hopes some bees may make a nest in it—then I should get the honey."[279]

"But you've got a bee-hive—or something like one—fastened to the saddle," said Alice.

"Yes, it's a very good bee-hive," the Knight said in a discontented tone, "one of the best kind. But not a single bee has come near it yet. And the other thing is a mouse-trap. I suppose the mice keep the bees out—or the bees keep the mice out, I don't know which."[280]

"I was wondering what the mouse-trap was for," said Alice. "It isn't very likely there would be any mice on the horse's back."

"Not very likely, perhaps,"[281] said the Knight; "but, if they *do* come, I don't choose to have them running all about.

278 *the box is no use without them*—a curious remark, as it would become useful again, if things were put in it again, and the lid properly closed. And to discard the box immediately rather than ensuring that the lid is properly fastened seems an unnecessary and over-hasty reaction.

279 One assumes that the Knight will add something to the box to denote his ownership of it—otherwise, any passer-by could claim the honey.

280 The Knight's thoughts are classic examples of "begging the question", and his comment on the bee-hive being a very good one reminds us of the March Hare's comment (when trying to mend the Hatter's watch) about the butter being the best butter. The quality of hive and butter are in no way relevant to their current proposed use.

281 *Not very likely, perhaps*—the Knight is responding literally to Alice's comment, which Alice has only made in order to be good-mannered.

"You see," he went on after a pause, "it's as well to be provided for *everything*. That's the reason the horse has all those anklets round his feet."

"But what are they for?" Alice asked in a tone of great curiosity.

"To guard against the bites of sharks,"[282] the Knight replied. "It's an invention of my own. And now help me on. I'll go with you to the end of the wood[283]——what's that dish for?"

"It's meant for plum-cake," said Alice.[284]

"We'd better take it with us," the Knight said. "It'll come in handy if we find any plum-cake. Help me to get it into this bag."

This took a long time to manage, though Alice held the bag open very carefully, because the Knight was so *very* awkward in putting in the dish:[285] the first two or three times that he tried he fell in himself instead. "It's rather a tight fit, you see," he said, as they got it in at last; "there are so many candlesticks in the bag." And he hung it to the saddle, which was already loaded with bunches of carrots, and fire-irons, and many other things.[286]

"I hope you've got your hair well fastened on?" he continued, as they set off.

"Only in the usual way," Alice said, smiling.

---

282 *To guard against the bites of sharks*—if we follow the Knight's ways of thinking, this is just as reasonable as the reasons he offers for the hive and mouse-trap.

283 *I'll go with you to the end of the wood*—the second time the Knight has said this—he is nothing if not chivalrous.

284 *It's meant for plum-cake*—the Knight takes this literally—though one would have thought it could be used for *any* comestibles.

285 In contrast to the occasion when Haigha removed the dish with ease from *his* bag, the Knight has great difficulty getting it into *his* bag.

286 Unlike the hive and mouse-trap, we are given no reason why the Knight should be carrying candlesticks, carrots, and fire-irons on his horse.

"That's hardly enough," he said, anxiously. "You see the wind is so *very* strong here. It's as strong as soup."[287]

"Have you invented a plan for keeping the hair from being blown off?" Alice inquired.

"Not yet," said the Knight. "But I've got a plan for keeping it from *falling* off."

"I should like to hear it, very much."

"First you take an upright stick," said the Knight. "Then you make your hair creep up it, like a fruit-tree.[288] Now the reason hair falls off is because it hangs *down*—things never fall *upwards,* you know. It's a plan of my own invention. You may try it if you like."

It didn't sound a comfortable plan, Alice thought, and for a few minutes she walked on in silence, puzzling over the idea, and every now and then stopping to help the poor Knight, who certainly was *not* a good rider.

Whenever the horse stopped (which it did very often), he fell off in front; and, whenever it went on again (which it generally did rather suddenly), he fell off behind. Otherwise he kept on pretty well, except that he had a habit of now and then falling off sideways; and, as he generally did this on the side on which Alice was walking, she soon found that it was the best plan not to walk *quite* close to the horse.

"I'm afraid you've not had much practice in riding," she ventured to say, as she was helping him up from his fifth tumble.

The Knight looked very much surprised, and a little offended at the remark. "What makes you say that?" he asked, as he scrambled back into the saddle, keeping hold of

---

287 *strong as soup*—in typical Carroll fashion, the Knight is using two quite different meanings for "strong".

288 He does not of course explain how you could possibly make hair creep up the stick.

Alice's hair with one hand,[289] to save himself from falling over on the other side.

"Because people don't fall off quite so often, when they've had much practice."

"I've had plenty of practice," the Knight said very gravely: "plenty of practice!"

Alice could think of nothing better to say than "Indeed?" but she said it as heartily as she could. They went on a little

289 *keeping hold of Alice's hair with one hand*—he now seems to have total confidence in this being effective in stopping him falling off—in contrast to his earlier thoughts that her hair was not safely 'fastened on'.

way in silence after this, the Knight with his eyes shut,[290] muttering to himself, and Alice watching anxiously for the next tumble.

The great art of riding," The Knight suddenly began in a loud voice, waving his right arm as he spoke, "is to keep——" here the sentence ended as suddenly as it had begun, as the Knight fell heavily on the top of his head exactly in the path where Alice was walking. She was quite frightened this time, and said in an anxious tone, as she picked him up, "I hope no bones are broken?"

"None to speak of," the Knight said, as if he didn't mind breaking two or three of them. "The great art of riding, as I was saying, is—to keep your balance properly. Like this, you know——"

He let go the bridle, ands stretched out both his arms to show Alice what he meant, and this time he fell flat on his back, right under the horse's feet.

"Plenty of practice!" he went on repeating, all the time that Alice was getting him on his feet again. "Plenty of practice!"

"It's too ridiculous!" cried Alice, losing all her patience this time. "You ought to have a wooden horse on wheels, that you ought!"

"Does that kind go smoothly?" the Knight asked in a tone of great interest, clasping his arms round the horse's neck as he spoke, just in time to save himself from tumbling off again.

"Much more smoothly than a live horse," Alice said, with a little scream of laughter, in spite of all she could do to prevent it.

"I'll get one," the Knight said thoughtfully to himself. "One or two—several."

There was a sort silence after this, and then the Knight went on again. "I'm a great hand at inventing things. Now,

290   *with his eyes shut*—we are not told why his eyes are shut.

I daresay you noticed, the last time you picked me up, that I was looking rather thoughtful?"

"You *were* a little grave," said Alice.

"Well, just then I was inventing a new way of getting over a gate—would you like to hear it?"

"Very much indeed," said Alice politely.

"I'll tell you how I came to think of it," said the Knight. "You see, I said to myself 'The only difficulty is with the feet: the *head* is high enough already.' Now, first I put my head on the top of the gate—then the head's high enough—then I stand on my head—then the feet are high enough, you see— then I'm over, you see."

"Yes, I suppose you'd be over when that was done," Alice said thoughtfully: "but don't you think it would be rather hard?"[291]

"I haven't tried it yet," the Knight said, gravely; "so I ca'n't tell for certain—but I'm afraid it *would* be a little hard."

He looked so vexed at the idea, that Alice changed the subject hastily. "What a curious helmet you've got!" she said cheerfully. "Is that your invention too?"

The Knight looked down proudly at his helmet, which hung from the saddle. "Yes," he said; "but I've invented a better one than that—like a sugar-loaf. When I used to wear it, if I fell off the horse, it always touched the ground directly. So I had a *very* little way to fall, you see—but there *was* the danger of falling *into* it, to be sure. That happened to me once—and the worst of it was, before I could get out again, the other White Knight came and put it on. He thought it was his own helmet."[292]

291 An incontrovertible point.

292 The Knight tells us that he invented his helmet. But a similar design (denoting the head of a horse) is also used by the Red Knight (or at least as they are portrayed by Tenniel)—so at least one of his inventions is right,

The Knight looked so solemn about it that Alice did not dare to laugh. "I'm afraid you must have hurt him," she said in a trembling voice, "being on the top of his head."

"I had to kick him, of course," the Knight said, very seriously. "And then he took the helmet off again—but it took hours and hours to get me out. I was as fast as—as lightning, you know."

"But that's a different kind of fastness," Alice objected.

The Knight shook his head. "It was all kinds of fastness with me, I can assure you!" he said. He raised his hands in some excitement as he said this, and instantly rolled out of the saddle, and fell headlong into a deep ditch.

Alice ran to the side of the ditch to look for him. She was rather startled by the fall, as for some time he had kept on very well, and she was afraid that he really *was* hurt this time. However, though she could see nothing but the soles of his feet, she was much relieved to hear that he was talking on in his usual tone. "All kinds of fastness," he repeated: "but it was careless of him to put another man's helmet on—with the man in it, too."

and useful, and used by other players in the game.

"How *can* you go on talking so quietly, head downwards?" Alice asked, as she dragged him out by the feet, and laid him in a heap on the bank.

The Knight looked surprised at the question. "What does it matter where my body happens to be?" he said. "My mind goes on working all the same. In fact, the more head-downwards I am, the more I keep inventing new things."

"Now the cleverest thing of the sort that I ever did," he went on after a pause, "was inventing a new pudding during the meat-course."

"In time to have it cooked for the next course?" said Alice. "Well, that *was* quick work, certainly!"

"Well, not the *next* course," the Knight said in a slow thoughtful tone: "no, certainly not the next *course*."[293]

"Then it would have to be the next day. I suppose you wouldn't have two pudding-courses in one dinner?"[294]

"Well, not the *next* day," the Knight repeated as before: "not the next *day*.[295] In fact," he went on, holding his head down, and his voice getting lower and lower, "I don't believe that pudding ever *was* cooked! In fact, I don't believe that pudding ever *will* be cooked! And yet it was a very clever pudding to invent."

"What did you mean it to be made of?" Alice asked, hoping to cheer him up, for the poor Knight seemed quite low-spirited about it.

"It began with blotting-paper," the Knight answered with a groan.

"That wouldn't be very nice, I'm afraid——"

293　*not the NEXT course… not the next COURSE*—the change of emphasis from "next" to "course" suggests that the new pudding might be intended for another part of the meal, or even to be eaten on its own, as it were.

294　Alice is responding to the first emphasis, rather than the second.

295　*the NEXT day… not the next DAY*—as with the previous changes of emphasis, the Knight appears to be suggesting that the pudding could have been consumed during the night.

"Not very nice *alone*," he interrupted, quite eagerly: "but you've no idea what a difference it makes, mixing it with other things—such as gunpowder and sealing-wax. And here I must leave you." They had just come to the end of the wood.

Alice could only look puzzled: she was thinking of the pudding.

"You are sad," the Knight said in an anxious tone: "let me sing you a song to comfort you."

"Is it very long?" Alice asked, for she had heard a good deal of poetry that day.

"It's long," said the Knight, "but it's very, *very* beautiful. Everybody that hears me sing it—either it brings the *tears* into their eyes, or else——"296

"Or else what?" said Alice, for the Knight had made a sudden pause.

"Or else it doesn't, you know. The name of the song is called '*Haddocks' Eyes*.'"

"Oh, that's the name of the song, is it?" Alice said, trying to feel interested.

"No, you don't understand," the Knight said, looking a little vexed. "That's what the name is *called*. The name really is '*The Aged Aged Man*.'"

"Then I ought to have said 'That's what the *song* is called'?" Alice corrected herself.

"No, you oughtn't: that's quite another thing! The *song* is called '*Ways And Means*': but that's only what it's *called* you know!"

"Well, what *is* the song, then?" said Alice, who was by this time completely bewildered.

"I was coming to that," the Knight said. "The song really is '*A-sitting On A Gate*': and the tune's my own invention."297

---

296   If it is designed to induce tears, it seems a strange song to sing when the Knight is only contemplating singing it because he thinks Alice is sad.

297   Our author has conceived a brilliantly original piece of dialogue. Even so,

So saying, he stopped his horse and let the reins fall on its neck: then, slowly beating time with one hand, and with a faint smile lighting up his gentle foolish face, as if he enjoyed the music of his song, he began.

Of all the strange things that Alice saw in her journey Through the Looking-Glass, this was the one that she always remembered most clearly. Years afterwards she could bring the whole scene back again, as if it had been only yesterday—the mild blue eyes and kindly smile of the Knight—the setting sun gleaming through his hair, and shining on his armour in a blaze of light that quite dazzled her—the horse quietly moving about, with the reins hanging loose on his neck,[298] cropping the grass at her feet—and the black shadows of the forest behind—all this she took in like a picture, as, with one hand shading her eyes, she leant against a tree, watching the strange pair, and listening, in a half-dream, to the melancholy music of the song.[299]

"But the tune *isn't* his own invention," she said to herself: "It's '*I give thee all, I can no more.*'" She stood and listened very attentively, but no tears came into her eyes.

> "*I'll tell thee everything I can:*
>   *There's little to relate.*
> *I saw an aged aged man,*
>   *A-sitting on a gate.*
> '*Who are you, aged man?*' *I said.*
>   '*And how is it you live?*'

Denis Crutch has pointed out that when it comes to—'The song really *is*... the Knight logically should really start straight into the song, rather than employ yet another name. (*The Annotated Alice* tells us that Roger W. Holmes made the same point ('The Philosopher's *Alice in Wonderland*: *The Antioch Review* Summer 1959).

298   The horse is perceived here as male, previously "he" was "it".

299   This paragraph, the longest in the book, has the most evocative and nostalgic feel, that we do not find anywhere else. It is little wonder that readers see the White Knight as reflecting Lewis Carroll himself.

And his answer trickled through my head,
Like water through a sieve.

He said 'I look for butterflies
That sleep among the wheat:
I make them into mutton-pies,
And sell them in the street.
I sell them unto men,' he said,
'Who sail on stormy seas;
And that's the way I get my bread—
A trifle, if you please.'

But I was thinking of a plan
To dye one's whiskers green,
And always use so large a fan
That they could not be seen.
So, having no reply to give
To what the old man said,
I cried 'Come, tell me how you live!'
And thumped him on the head.

His accents mild took up the tale:
He said 'I go my ways,
And when I find a mountain-rill,
I set it in a blaze;
And thence they make a stuff they call
Rowland's Macassar-Oil—
Yet twopence-halfpenny is all
They give me for my toil.'

But I was thinking of a way
To feed oneself on batter,
And so go on from day to day
Getting a little fatter

I shook him well from side to side,
Until his face was blue:
'Come, tell me how you live,' I cried,
'And what it is you do!'

He said 'I hunt for haddocks' eyes
Among the heather bright,
And work them into waistcoat-buttons
In the silent night.
And these I do not sell for gold
Or coin of silvery shine,
But for a copper halfpenny,
And that will purchase nine.

'I sometimes dig for buttered rolls,
Or set limed twigs for crabs:
I sometimes search the grassy knolls
For wheels of Hansom-cabs.

And that's the way' (he gave a wink)
'By which I get my wealth—
And very gladly will I drink
Your Honour's noble health.'

I heard him then, for I had just
Completed my design
To keep the Menai bridge from rust
By boiling it in wine.
I thanked him much for telling me
The way he got his wealth,
But chiefly for his wish that he
Might drink my noble health.

And now, if e'er by chance I put
My fingers into glue,
Or madly squeeze a right-hand foot
Into a left-hand shoe,
Of if I drop upon my toe
A very heavy weight,
I weep, for it reminds me so
Of that old man I used to know—
Whose look was mild, whose speech was slow,
Whose hair was whiter than the snow,
Whose face was very like a crow,
With eyes, like cinders, all aglow,
Who seemed distracted with his woe,
Who rocked his body to and fro,
And muttered mumblingly and low,
As if his mouth were full of dough,
Who snorted like a buffalo——
That summer evening long ago,
A-sitting on a gate."

As the Knight sang the last words of the ballad,[300] he gathered up the reins, and turned his horse's head along the road by which they had come. "You've only a few yards to go," he said, "down the hill and over that little brook, and then you'll be a Queen——but you'll stay and see me off first?" he added as Alice turned with an eager look in the direction to which he pointed, "I sha'n't be long. You'll wait and wave your handkerchief when I get to that turn in the road? I think it will encourage me, you see."

"Of course I'll wait," said Alice: "and thank you very much for coming so far—and for the song—I liked it very much."

"I hope so," the Knight said doubtfully: "but you didn't cry so much as I thought you would."[301]

So they shook hands, and then the Knight rode slowly away into the forest. "It wo'n't take long to see him *off*,[302] I expect," Alice said to herself, as she stood watching him. "There he goes! Right on his head as usual! However, he gets on again pretty easily—that comes of having so many things hung round the horse——" so she went on talking to herself, as she watched the horse walking leisurely along the road, and the Knight tumbling off, first on one side and then on the other. After the fourth or fifth tumble he reached the turn, and then she waved her handkerchief to him, and waited till he was out of sight.

"I hope it encouraged him," she said, as she turned to run down the hill: "and now for the last brook, and to be a Queen! How grand it sounds!" A very few steps brought her to the edge of the brook. "The Eighth Square at last!" she cried, as she bounded across,

---

300 *the ballad*—this is the first time the poem has been described as a ballad. The White Knight earlier only spoke of it as a song.

301 Again, a slightly odd remark in that he had originally proposed singing the song to cheer Alice up.

302 *see him off*—Alice allows herself a little joke.

and threw herself down to rest on a lawn as soft as moss, with little flower-beds dotted about it here and there. "Oh, how glad I am to get here! And what *is* this on my head?" she exclaimed in a tone of dismay, as she put her hands up to something very heavy, that fitted tight all round her head.

"But how *can* it have got there without my knowing it?" she said to herself, as she lifted it off, and set it on her lap to make out what it could possibly be.

It was a golden crown.

INTRODUCTION TO CHAPTER IX

*O*nce more, Alice is alone at the end of the preceding chapter. We look forward with some anticipation to what happens now Alice is a Queen. We have already met both the White Queen and the Red Queen, with their very different personalities. Now for the first time we are destined to meet them together.

This is the longest chapter in the book, and takes us from the confrontation with the Queens, straight into the feast with its violent apocalyptic climax.

CHAPTER IX

Queen Alice

"Well, this *is* grand!" said Alice. "I never expected I
should be a Queen so soon—and I'll tell you what it
is, your Majesty," she went on, in a severe tone (she was
always rather fond of scolding herself), "it'll never do for you
to be lolling about on the grass like that! Queens have to be
dignified, you know!"

So she got up and walked about—rather stiffly just at first,
as she was afraid that the crown might come off: but she
comforted herself with the thought that there was nobody to
see her, "and if I really am a Queen," she said as she sat
down again, "I shall be able to manage it quite well in time."

Everything was happening so oddly that she didn't feel a
bit surprised at finding the Red Queen and the White Queen
sitting close to her,[303] one on each side: she would have liked
very much to ask them how they came there, but she feared
it would not be quite civil. However, there would be no harm,

303 *finding the Red Queen and the White Queen sitting close to her*—another
instance of the sudden appearance from nowhere of characters—a now
familiar occurrence in the book.

she thought, in asking if the game was over. "Please, would you tell me——" she began, looking timidly at the Red Queen.

"Speak when you're spoken to!" the Queen sharply interrupted her.

"But if everybody obeyed that rule," said Alice, who was always ready for a little argument, "and if you only spoke when you were spoken to, and the other person always waited for *you* to begin, you see nobody would ever say anything, so that——"[304]

304 In "answering back" to the Red Queen, Alice has subconsciously assumed the role of Queen—at their first meeting in Chapter II, she would never have dared to argue back in this way.

"Ridiculous!" cried the Queen. "Why, don't you see, child——"[305] here she broke off[306] with a frown, and, after thinking for a minute, suddenly changed the subject of the conversation. "What do you mean by 'If you really are a Queen'?[307] What right have you to call yourself so? You ca'n't be a Queen,[308] you know, till you've passed the proper examination. And the sooner we begin it, the better."

"I only said 'if'!" poor Alice pleaded in a piteous tone.

The two Queens looked at each other, and the Red Queen remarked, with a little shudder, "She *says* she only said 'if'——"

"But she said a great deal more than that!" the White Queen moaned, wringing her hands. "Oh, ever so much more than that!"[309]

"So you did, you know," the Red Queen said to Alice. "Always speak the truth—think before you speak—and write it down afterwards."

"I'm sure I didn't mean——" Alice was beginning, but the Red Queen interrupted her impatiently.

"That's just what I complain of! You *should* have meant! What do you suppose is the use of a child without any meaning? Even a joke should have some meaning—and a child's more important than a joke, I hope. You couldn't deny that, even if you tried with both hands."[310]

305   The Red Queen addresses Alice as "child"—so it is understandable that she fails to appreciate Alice's newly royal status.

306   *here she broke off*—understandably, as Alice's comment is undeniable.

307   *'If you really are a Queen'*—our author has put this in inverted commas, but this is surely wrong, as it is reported speech—they are not the precise words that Alice had used—she said "and if I really am a Queen".

308   *You ca'n't be a Queen*—belied by our deus ex machina which has already crowned her.

309   The White Queen is surely exaggerating a little.

310   The Queen is of course being very unfair. When Alice said "I didn't mean... ."—she was not referring to personal status, but to the interpretation of

"I don't deny things with my *hands*," Alice objected.

"Nobody said you did," said the Red Queen. "I said you couldn't if you tried."

"She's in that state of mind," said the White Queen, "that she wants to deny *something*—only she doesn't know what to deny!"[311]

"A nasty, vicious temper," the Red Queen remarked; and there was an uncomfortable silence for a minute or two.

The Red Queen broke the silence by saying, to the White Queen, "I invite you to Alice's dinner-party this afternoon."

The White Queen smiled feebly and said "And I invite *you*."

"I didn't know I was to have a party at all," said Alice; "but, if there *is* to be one, I think *I* ought to invite the guests."

"We gave you the opportunity of doing it," the Red Queen remarked: "but I daresay you've not had many lessons in manners yet?"[312]

"Manners are not taught in lessons," said Alice. "Lessons teach you to do sums, and things of that sort."[313]

"Can you do Addition?" the White Queen asked. "What's one and one and one and one and one and one and one and one and one and one?"

"I don't know," said Alice. "I lost count."[314]

"She ca'n't do Addition," the Red Queen interrupted. "Can you do Subtraction? Take nine from eight."

---

her earlier remark.

311 Again this is unfair to Alice, who only commented on denying anything in response to the Red Queen's statement.

312 Quite when the opportunity was available is not vouchsafed.

313 Alice appears to have accepted the reproof that she has missed her chance to issue invitations. Her mention of "sums" stimulates the Queens to start the examination with "sums".

314 The answer of course is "ten"—one does wonder whether the White Queen has kept count herself—but Alice does not challenge her as to the correct answer.

"Nine from eight I ca'n't, you know," Alice replied very readily: "but——"[315]

"She ca'n't do Subtraction," said the White Queen. "Can you do Division? Divide a loaf by a knife—what's the answer to *that?*"

"I suppose——" Alice was beginning, but the Red Queen answered for her. "Bread-and-butter, of course. Try another Subtraction sum. Take a bone from a dog: what remains?"[316]

Alice considered. "The bone wouldn't remain, of course, if I took it—and the dog wouldn't remain: it would come to bite me—and I'm sure *I* shouldn't remain!"[317]

---

315   It is interesting that Alice has not learnt about minus, or negative, numbers in her schooling, though one does wonder what she was about to say, before being interrupted.

316   Again we do not know what Alice was about to say, as she is interrupted so abruptly. The Red Queen's answer is the first that has been offered to any of the questions so far asked. She now returns to an earlier subject.

317   Alice is now entering into the spirit of the examination, and is happy to make a stab at a satisfactory answer.

"Then you think nothing would remain?" said the Red Queen.

"I think that's the answer."

"Wrong, as usual," said the Red Queen: "the dog's temper would remain."

"But I don't see how——"

"Why, look here!" the Red Queen cried. "The dog would lose its temper, wouldn't it?"

"Perhaps it would," Alice replied cautiously.

"Then if the dog went away, its temper would remain!" the Queen exclaimed triumphantly.

Alice said, as gravely as she could,[318] "They might go different ways." But she couldn't help thinking to herself "What dreadful nonsense we *are* talking!"

"She ca'n't do sums a *bit!*" the Queens said together, with great emphasis.

"Can *you* do sums?" Alice said, turning suddenly on the White Queen, for she didn't like being found fault with so much.[319]

The Queen gasped and shut her eyes. "I can do Addition," she said, "if you give me time—but I ca'n't do Subtraction under *any* circumstances!"[320]

"Of course you know your ABC?" said the Red Queen.

"To be sure I do" said Alice.

"So do I," the White Queen whispered: "we'll often say it over together, dear. And I'll tell you a secret—I can read

318 *as gravely as she could*—suggests that she is trying to stop herself laughing—her reply is of course incontrovertible.

319 Alice turns on the White Queen rather than the Red Queen, as a softer target.

320 Which makes one wonder how *she* came to qualify for the role of Queen, as Alice has been told she cannot be a Queen until she has passed the 'proper examination'. But of course the Queen was always a queen, whereas Alice has been created one in response to reaching the Eighth Square.

words of one letter![321] Isn't *that* grand? However, don't be discouraged. You'll come to it in time."

Here the Red Queen began again. "Can you answer useful questions?" she said. "How is bread made?"

"I know *that!*" Alice cried eagerly. "You take some flour——"

"Where do you pick the flower?" The White Queen asked. "In a garden or in the hedges?"

"Well, it isn't *picked* at all," Alice explained: "it's *ground*——"

"How many acres of ground?" said the White Queen. "You mustn't leave out so many things."[322]

"Fan her head!" the Red Queen anxiously interrupted. "She'll be feverish after so much thinking." So they set to work and fanned her with bunches of leaves, till she had to beg them to leave off, it blew her hair about so.

"She's all right again now," said the Red Queen. "Do you know Languages? What's the French for fiddle-de-dee?"

"Fiddle-de-dee's not English," Alice replied gravely.[323]

"Whoever said it was?" said the Red Queen.

Alice thought she saw a way out of the difficulty, this time. "If you'll tell me what language 'fiddle-de-dee' is, I'll tell you the French for it!" she exclaimed triumphantly.

But the Queen drew herself up rather stiffly, and said "Queens never make bargains."

"I wish Queens never asked questions," Alice thought to herself.

"Don't let us quarrel," the White Queen said in an anxious tone. "What is the cause of lightning?"

---

321   *words of one letter*—are there any besides the word "a" and "I" and possibly "o"?

322   It is a little unfair of the Queen to complain that Alice is leaving things out, as she constantly interrupts Alice when Alice is in the middle of her answers.

323   But surely it is?

"The cause of lightning," Alice said very decidedly, for she felt quite certain about this, "is the thunder—no, no!" she hastily corrected herself. "I meant the other way."

"It's too late to correct it," said the Red Queen: "when you've once said a thing, that fixes it, and you must take the consequences."[324]

"Which reminds me——" the White Queen said, looking down and nervously clasping and unclasping her hands, "we had *such* a thunderstorm last Tuesday—I mean one of the last set of Tuesdays, you know."

Alice was puzzled. "In *our* country," she remarked, "there's only one day at a time."

The Red Queen said "That's a poor thin way of doing things, Now *here*, we mostly have days and nights two or three at a time, and sometimes in the winter we take as many as five nights together—for warmth, you know."

"Are five nights warmer than one night, then?" Alice ventured to ask.

"Five times as warm, of course."

"But they should be five times as *cold*, by the same rule——"

"Just so!" cried the Red Queen. "Five times as warm, *and* five times as cold—just as I'm five times as rich as you are, *and* five times as clever!"[325]

Alice sighed and gave it up. "It's exactly like a riddle with no answer!" she thought.

"Humpty Dumpty saw it too," the White Queen went on in a low voice, more as if she were talking to herself. "He came to the door with a corkscrew in his hand——"

"What did he want?" said the Red Queen.

---

324 Is this a reference to the game of chess? If you touch a piece when it is your turn, then you must move that piece, unless you say "J'adoube".

325 In the *The Annotated Alice* it is pointed out that the Queen is implying that "rich" and "clever" are opposites like "warm" and "cold".

"He said he *would* come in," the White Queen went on, "because he was looking for a hippopotamus.[326] Now, as it happened, there wasn't such a thing in the house, that morning."

"Is there generally?" Alice asked in an astonished tone.

"Well, only on Thursdays," said the Queen.

"I know what he came for," said Alice: "he wanted to punish the fish, because——"[327]

Here the White Queen began again. "It was *such* a thunderstorm, you ca'n't think!" ("She *never* could, you know," said the Red Queen.) "And part of the roof came off, and ever so much thunder got in—and it went rolling round the room in great lumps—and knocking over the tables and things—till I was so frightened, I couldn't remember my own name!"

Alice thought to herself "I never should *try* to remember my name in the middle of an accident! Where would be the use of it?" but she did not say this aloud, for fear of hurting the poor Queen's feelings.

"Your Majesty[328] must excuse her," the Red Queen said to Alice, taking one of the White Queen's hands in her own, and gently stroking it: "she means well, but she ca'n't help saying foolish things, as a general rule."

The White Queen looked timidly at Alice, who felt she *ought* to say something kind, but really couldn't think of anything at the moment.

---

326 If the Queen is referring to Humpty Dumpty's poem—then he had the corkscrew to help him wake up the fishes in bed, rather than in looking for a hippopotamus.

327 Alice is interrupted, so we do not know if she really knew why Humpty wanted to punish the fish—it was not made clear at all in his poem, where the fault lay. Did Alice know more? We never find out.

328 *Your Majesty*—it would appear that the Red Queen now accepts Alice as a Queen, so she must have been successful in the examination.

"She never was really well brought up," the Red Queen went on: "but it's amazing how good-tempered she is! Pat her on the head, and see how pleased she'll be!" But this was more than Alice had courage to do.[329]

"A little kindness and putting her hair in papers—would do wonders with her——"

The White Queen gave a deep sigh, and laid her head on Alice's shoulder. "I *am* so sleepy!" she moaned.

"She's tired, poor thing!" said the Red Queen. "Smoothe her hair—lend her your nightcap—and sing her a soothing lullaby."

"I haven't got a nightcap with me," said Alice, as she tried to obey the first direction: "and I don't know any soothing lullabies."

"I must do it myself, then," said the Red Queen, and she began:—

> *"Hush-a-by lady, in Alice's lap!*
> *Till the feast's ready, we've time for a nap.*
> *When the feast's over, we'll go to the ball—*
> *Red Queen, and White Queen, and Alice, and all!*

"And now you know the words," she added, as she put her head down on Alice's other shoulder, "just sing it through to *me*. I'm getting sleepy, too." In another moment both Queens were fast asleep, and snoring loud.

"What *am* I to do?" exclaimed Alice, looking about in great perplexity, as first one round head, and then the other, rolled down from her shoulder, and lay like a heavy lump in her lap. "I don't think it *ever* happened before, that any one had to take care of two Queens asleep at once! No, not in all the History of England—it couldn't, you know, because there

329 The Red Queen's attitude towards the White Queen has quite suddenly changed from that of a colleague to a generally patronizing approach.

never was more than one Queen at a time. Do wake up, you heavy things!" she went on in an impatient tone; but there was no answer but a gentle snoring.[330]

The snoring got more distinct every minute, and sounded more like a tune: at last she could even make out words,[331] and she listened so eagerly that, when the two great heads suddenly vanished from her lap, she hardly missed them.

She was standing before an arched doorway, over which were the words "QUEEN ALICE" in large letters, and on each side of the arch there was a bell-handle; one was marked "Visitors' Bell," and the other "Servants' Bell,"[332]

"I'll wait till the song's over," thought Alice, "and then I'll ring the—the—*which* bell must I ring?" she went on, very much puzzled by the names. "I'm not a visitor, and I'm not a servant. There *ought* to be one marked 'Queen,' you know——"

---

330   *gentle snoring*—earlier it was described as loud.

331   *sounded more like a tune....she could even make out words*—one wonders if our author was originally going to tell us what the words were, but then got more interested in developing the plot in other directions.

332   It has been pointed out that as we are in Looking-Glass Land, these words should really be in "mirror writing".

Just then the door opened a little way, and a creature with a long beak put its head out for a moment and said "No admittance till the week after next!" and shut the door again with a bang.

Alice knocked and rang in vain for a long time; but at last a very old Frog, who was sitting under a tree, got up and hobbled slowly towards her: he was dressed in bright yellow, and had enormous boots on.

"What is it, now?" the Frog said in a deep hoarse whisper.

Alice turned round, ready to find fault with anybody. "Where's the servant whose business it is to answer the door?" she began angrily.

"Which door?" said the Frog.

Alice almost stamped with irritation at the slow drawl in which he spoke. "*This* door, of course!"

The Frog looked at the door with his large dull eyes for a minute: then he went nearer and rubbed it with his thumb, as if he were trying whether the paint would come off: then he looked at Alice.

"To answer the door?" he said. "What's it been asking of?" He was so hoarse that Alice could scarcely hear him.

"I don't know what you mean," she said.

"I speaks English, doesn't I?" the Frog went on. "Or are you deaf? What did it ask you?"

"Nothing!" Alice said impatiently. "I've been knocking at it!"

"Shouldn't do that—shouldn't do that——" the Frog muttered. "Wexes it, you know." Then he went up and gave the door a kick with one of his great feet.[333] "You let *it* alone," he panted out, as he hobbled back to his tree, "and it'll let *you* alone, you know."[334]

At this moment the door was flung open, and a shrill voice was heard singing:—

"To the Looking-Glass world[335] *it was Alice that said*
'I've a sceptre in hand I've a crown on my head.
Let the Looking-Glass creatures whatever they be
Come and dine with the Red Queen, the White Queen, and
     me!'"

---

333 *gave the door a kick with one his great feet*—a curious reaction, since he has just criticized Alice for simply knocking on the door.

334 This whole brilliant dialogue reminds us of the Frog Footman in *Alice's Adventures in Wonderland*, where a quite different conversation takes place concerning the process of knocking at a door. This Frog Footman speaks in a working class fashion, with elements of cockney ("Wexes it"—reminds us a little of Sam Weller in *Pickwick Papers*—as pointed out in *The Annotated Alice*).

335 *Looking-Glass world*—this is the first time anyone in Looking-Glass world has actually called it that.

And hundreds of voices joined in the chorus:—

"Then fill up the glasses as quick as you can,
And sprinkle the table with buttons and bran:
Put cats in the coffee, and mice in the tea—
And welcome Queen Alice with thirty-times-three!"

Then followed a confused noise of cheering, and Alice thought to herself "Thirty times three makes ninety. I wonder if any one's counting?" In a minute there was silence again, and the same shrill voice sang another verse:—

"'O Looking-Glass creatures,' quoth Alice, 'draw near!
'Tis an honour to see me, a favour to hear:
'Tis a privilege high to have dinner and tea
Along with the Red Queen, the White Queen, and me!'"

Then came the chorus again:—

"Then fill up the glasses with treacle and ink,
Or anything else that is pleasant to drink:
Mix sand with the cider, and wool with the wine—
And welcome Queen Alice with ninety-times-nine!"

"Ninety times nine!" Alice repeated in despair. "Oh, that'll never be done! I'd better go in at once——" and in she went, and there was a dead silence the moment she appeared.

Alice glanced nervously along the table, as she walked up the large hall, and noticed that there were about fifty guests, of all kinds: some were animals, some birds, and there were even a few flowers among them. "I'm glad they've come without waiting to be asked," she thought: "I should never have known who were the right people to invite!"

There were three chairs at the head of the table: the Red and White Queens had already taken two of them, but the middle one was empty. Alice sat down in it, rather uncomfortable at the silence, and longing for some one to speak.

At last the Red Queen began. "You've missed the soup and fish," she said. "Put on the joint!" And the waiters set a leg of mutton before Alice, who looked at it rather anxiously, as she had never had to carve a joint before.

"You look a little shy: let me introduce you to that leg of mutton," said the Red Queen. "Alice——Mutton: Mutton——Alice." The leg of mutton got up in the dish and made a little bow to Alice; and Alice returned the bow, not knowing whether to be frightened or amused.[336]

336 One wonders whether the soup and fish that Alice had missed had also taken on anthropological personae.

"May I give you a slice?" she said, taking up the knife and fork, and looking from one Queen to the other.

"Certainly not," the Red Queen said, very decidedly: "it isn't etiquette to cut any one you've been introduced to. Remove the joint!" And the waiters carried it off, and brought a large plum-pudding in its place.

"I wo'n't be introduced to the pudding, please," Alice said rather hastily, "or we shall get no dinner at all. May I give you some?"

But the Red Queen looked sulky, and growled "Pudding——Alice: Alice——Pudding. Remove the pudding!", and the waiters took it away so quickly that Alice couldn't return its bow.

However, she didn't see why the Red Queen should be the only one to give orders; so, as an experiment, she called out "Waiter! Bring back the pudding!", and there it was again in a moment, like a conjuring-trick. It was so large that she couldn't help feeling a *little* shy with it, as she had been with the mutton: however, she conquered her shyness by a great effort, and cut a slice and handed it to the Red Queen.

"What impertinence!" said the Pudding. "I wonder how you'd like it, if I were to cut a slice out of *you*, you creature!"

It spoke in a thick, suety[337] sort of voice, and Alice hadn't a word to say in reply: she could only sit and look at it and gasp.

"Make a remark," said the Red Queen: "it's ridiculous to leave all the conversation to the pudding!"[338]

"Do you know, I've had such a quantity of poetry repeated to me to-day," Alice began, a little frightened at finding that, the moment she opened her lips, there was dead silence, and

---

337 *suety*—must be a word created by Lewis Carroll—one cannot imagine any other scenario where such a word would be needed.

338 The Red Queen seems to have accepted Alice's right to cut into the pudding, she now only wishes the proper social graces to be observed.

all eyes were fixed upon her; "and it's a very curious thing, I think—every poem was about fishes in some way.[339] Do you know why they're so fond of fishes, all about here?"

She spoke to the Red Queen, whose answer was a little wide of the mark. "As to fishes," she said, very slowly and solemnly, putting her mouth close to Alice's ear, "her White Majesty knows a lovely riddle—all in poetry—all about fishes. Shall she repeat it?"

"Her Red Majesty's very kind to mention it," the White Queen murmured into Alice's other ear, in a voice like the cooing of a pigeon. "It would be *such* a treat! May I?"

"Please do," Alice said very politely.

The White Queen laughed with delight, and stroked Alice's cheek. Then she began:—

> *"'First, the fish must be caught.'*
> *That is easy: a baby, I think, could have caught it.*
> *'Next, the fish must be bought.'*
> *That is easy: a penny, I think, would have bought it.*
>
> *'Now cook me the fish!'*
> *That is easy, and will not take more than a minute.*
> *'Let it lie in a dish!'*
> *That is easy, because it already is in it.*
>
> *'Bring it here! Let me sup!'*
> *It is easy to set such a dish on the table.*
> *Take the dish-cover up!'*
> *Ah, that is so hard that I fear I'm unable!*

---

339   *every poem was about fishes in some way*—hardly true really. *The Walrus and the Carpenter* does not mention fish (unless you consider oysters to be fish-related), nor does the White Knight's song (except for the single phrase 'haddocks' eyes'—which hardly makes the poem 'about fishes').

For it holds it like glue—
Holds the lid to the dish, while it lies in the middle:
Which is easiest to do,
Un-dish-cover the fish, or dishcover the riddle?"

"Take a minute to think about it, and then guess," said the Red Queen. "Meanwhile, we'll drink your health—Queen Alice's health!" she screamed at the top of her voice, and all the guests began drinking it directly, and very queerly they managed it: some of them put their glasses upon their heads like extinguishers,[340] and drank all that trickled down their faces—others upset the decanters, and drank the wine as it ran off the edges of the table—and three of them (who looked like kangaroos) scrambled into the dish of roast mutton,[341] and began eagerly lapping up the gravy, "just lie pigs in a trough!" thought Alice.

"You ought to return thanks in a neat speech," the Red Queen said, frowning at Alice as she spoke.

"We must support you, you know," the White Queen whispered, as Alice got up to do it, very obediently, but a little frightened.

"Thank you very much," she whispered in reply, "but I can do quite well without."

"That wouldn't be at all the right thing," the Red Queen said very decidedly: so Alice tried to submit to it with a good grace.

("And they *did* push so!" she said afterwards, when she was telling her sister[342] the history of the feast. "You would have thought they wanted to squeeze me flat!")

---

340 *extinguishers*—our author is referring to extinguishers used to put out candle flames.

341 *dish of roast mutton*—this appears still to be on the table, in spite of the instruction to waiters earlier to 'remove the joint'.

342 *telling her sister*—as with her relating the meeting with the Tweedles in Chapter IV this again would appear to be the elder sister, who played such a prominent role in *Alice's Adventures in Wonderland*, rather than the younger (?) sister who is mentioned in Chapter I.

In fact it was rather difficult for her to keep her place while she made her speech: the two Queens pushed her so, one on each side, that they nearly lifted her up into the air. "I rise to return thanks——" Alice began: and she really *did* rise as she spoke, several inches; but she got hold of the edge of the table, and managed to pull herself down again.

"Take care of yourself!" screamed the White Queen, seizing Alice's hair with both her hands. "Something's going to happen!"

And then (as Alice afterwards described it) all sorts of things happened in a moment. The candles all grew up to the ceiling, looking something like a bed of rushes with fireworks at the top. As to the bottles, they each took a pair of plates, which they hastily fitted on as wings, and so, with forks for legs, went fluttering about in all directions: "and very like birds they look," Alice thought to herself, as well as she could in the dreadful confusion that was beginning.

At this moment she heard a hoarse laugh at her side, and turned to see what was the matter with the White Queen; but, instead of the Queen, there was the leg of mutton sitting in the chair. "Here I am!" cried a voice from the soup-tureen, and Alice turned again, just in time to see the Queen's broad good-natured face grinning at her for a moment over the edge of the tureen, before she disappeared into the soup.

There was not a moment to be lost. Already several of the guests were lying down in the dishes, and the soup-ladle was walking up the table towards Alice's chair, and beckoning to her impatiently to get out of its way.[343]

"I ca'n't stand this any longer!" she cried, as she jumped up and seized the table-cloth with both hands: one good pull, and plates, dishes, guests, and candles came crashing down together in a heap on the floor.

343 Was the soup-ladle intending to rescue the White Queen from drowning in the soup?

"And as for *you*," she went on, turning fiercely upon the Red Queen, whom she considered as the cause of all the mischief—but the Queen was no longer at her side—she had suddenly dwindled down to the size of a little doll, and was now on the table, merrily running round and round after her own shawl, which was trailing behind her.

At any other time, Alice would have felt surprised at this, but she was far too much excited to be surprised at anything *now*. "As for *you*," she repeated, catching hold of the little creature in the very act of jumping over a bottle which had just lighted upon the table, "I'll shake you into a kitten, that I will!"

INTRODUCTION TO CHAPTER X

This chapter would never be allowed in a modern children's book—as it encourages the shaking of a small creature (or child) in a violent way that would now be considered to be highly dangerous, and in no way to be encouraged.

CHAPTER **X**

Shaking

She took her off the table as she spoke, and shook her backwards and forwards with all her might.

The Red Queen made no resistance whatever: only her face grew very small, and her eyes got large and green: and still, as Alice went on shaking her, she kept on growing shorter—and fatter—and softer—and rounder—and——

x

INTRODUCTION TO CHAPTER XI

*T*his and the preceding chapter are a delightful amusing joke about the structure of chapters. The words are given added point in the original Macmillan editions with the facing page having a picture of the Queen's gradual transformation back into the kitten.

CHAPTER **XI**

Waking

—————*A*nd it really *was* a kitten, after all.

INTRODUCTION TO CHAPTER XII

*T*he final chapter brings a most satisfactory closure to the story. Some respite is indeed necessary after the violent conclusion to the feast. In a charmingly tranquil conclusion we return to the scene at the beginning of the book, with Alice alone with the two kittens.

Which Dreamed It?

"Your Red Majesty shouldn't purr so loud," Alice said, rubbing her eyes, and addressing the kitten, respectfully, yet with some severity. "You woke me out of oh! Such a nice dream! And you've been along with me, Kitty—all through the Looking-Glass world. Did you know it, dear?"

It is a very inconvenient habit of kittens (Alice had once made the remark) that, whatever you say to them, they *always* purr. "If they would only purr for 'yes,' and mew for 'no,' or any rule of that sort," she had said, "so that one could keep up a conversation! But how *can* you talk with a person if they *always* say the same thing?"

On this occasion the kitten only purred: and it was impossible to guess whether it meant "yes" or "no".

So Alice hunted among the chessmen on the table till she found the Red Queen: then she went down on her knees on the hearth-rug, and put the kitten and the Queen to look at each other. "Now, Kitty!" she cried, clapping her hands triumphantly. "Confess that was what turned into!"

("But it wouldn't look at it," she said, when she was explaining the thing afterwards to her sister: "it turned away its head, and pretended not to see it: but it looked a *little* ashamed of itself, so I think it *must* have been the Red Queen.")[344]

"Sit up a little more stiffly, dear!" Alice cried with a merry laugh. "And curtsey while you're thinking what to—what to purr. It saves time, remember!" And she caught it up and gave it one little kiss, "just in honour of having been a Red Queen."

344 As in Chapter I, Kitty remains neuter, in spite of her being obviously female. Curiously the chess piece Red Queen is also seen as neuter.

"Snowdrop, my pet!" she went on, looking over her shoulder at the White Kitten, which was still patiently undergoing its[345] toilet, "when *will* Dinah have finished with your White Majesty, I wonder? That must be the reason you were so untidy in my dream.——Dinah! Do you know that you're scrubbing a White Queen? Really, it's most disrespectful of you!

"And what did *Dinah* turn to, I wonder?" she prattled on, as she settled comfortably down, with one elbow on the rug, and her chin in her hand, to watch the kittens. "Tell me, Dinah, did you turn to Humpty Dumpty?[346] I *think* you did—however, you'd better not mention it to your friends just yet, for I'm not sure.[347]

"By the way, Kitty, if only you'd been really with me in my dream, there was one thing you *would* have enjoyed——I had such a quantity of poetry[348] said to me, all about fishes! To-morrow morning you shall have a real treat. All the time you're eating your breakfast, I'll repeat '*The Walrus and the Carpenter*' to you;[349] and then you can make believe it's oysters, dear!

"Now, Kitty, let's consider who it was that dreamed it all. This is a serious question, my dear, and you should *not* go on licking your paw like that—as if Dinah hadn't washed you this morning! You see Kitty, it *must* have been either me or

345 Snowdrop, unlike in Chapter I is now demoted to neuter.

346 *turn to Humpty Dumpty*—simply implies turning towards Humpty Dumpty. Was our author intending to say "turn into Humpty Dumpty"?

347 In *The Annotated Alice* it is rightly asked why Alice should wonder about Dinah turning into Humpty Dumpty—such a thought seems to have no relevance to the story at all. See *The Annotated Alice* for possible reasons.

348 *such a quantity of poetry, all about fishes*- as we affirmed earlier that this is not actually true—"*The Walrus and the Carpenter*" and the White Knight's song do not mention fish.

349 We can only pay tribute to Alice's powers of remembering—to be able to repeat the whole poem after hearing only the one rendition.

the Red King. He was part of my dream, of course—but then I was part of his dream, too![350] *Was* it the Red King, Kitty? You were his wife, my dear, so you ought to know——oh, Kitty, *do* help to settle it! I'm sure your paw can wait!" But the provoking kitten only began on the other paw, and pretended it hadn't heard the question.

Which do *you* think it was?[351]

---

350   Alice says that she was part of the Red King's dream, but this was only surmise by the Tweedles—see my note in Chapter IV for my reservations.

351   The fifth time the reader has been addressed directly.

A boat, beneath a sunny sky
Lingering onward dreamily
In an evening of July—

Children three that nestle near,
Eager eye and willing ear,
Pleased a simple tale to hear—

Long has paled that sunny sky:
Echoes fade and memories die:
Autumn frosts have slain July.

Still she haunts me, phantomwise,
Alice moving under skies
Never seen by waking eyes.

Children yet, the tale to hear
Eager eye and willing ear,
Lovingly shall nestle near.

In a Wonderland they lie,
Dreaming as the days go by,
Dreaming as the summers die:

Ever drifting down the stream—
Lingering in the golden gleam—
Life, what is it but a dream?

THE END.[352]

---

352 The final poem is included as part of the story. Our author only announces
"The End" *after* the poem. Is Carroll intending it to be the answer to
Alice's question?

CHRISTMAS GREETINGS

(FROM A FAIRY TO A CHILD)

Lady dear, if Fairies may
For a moment lay aside
Cunning tricks and elfish play,
'Tis at happy Christmas-tide.

We have heard the children say—
Gentle children, whom we love—
Long ago, on Christmas-Day,
Came a message from above.

Still, as Christmas-tide comes round,
They remember it again—
Echo still the joyful sound
"Peace on earth, good-will to men!"

Yet the hearts must childlike be
*   Where such heavenly guests abide:*
Unto children, in their glee,
*   All the year is Christmas-tide.*

Thus, forgetting tricks and play
*   For a moment, Lady dear,*
We would wish you, if we may,
*   Merry Christmas, glad New Year!*

*   Lewis Carroll*
*   Christmas, 1867.*

TO ALL CHILD READERS OF
Alice's Adventures in Wonderland

DEAR CHILDREN,

At Christmas time a few grave words are not quite out of place, I hope, even at the end of a book of nonsense—and I want to take this opportunity of thanking the thousands of children who have read "Alice's Adventures in Wonderland," for the kindly interest they have taken in my little dream-child.

The thought of the many English firesides where happy faces have smiled her a welcome, and of the many English children to whom she has brought an hour of (I trust) innocent amusement, is one of the brightest and pleasantest thoughts of my life. I have a host of young friends already, whose names and faces I know—but I cannot help feeling as if, through "Alice's Adventures," I had made friends with many many other dear children, whose faces I shall never see.

To all my little friends, known and unknown, I wish with all my heart, "A Merry Christmas and a Happy New Year." May God bless you, dear children, and make each Christmas-tide, as it comes round to you, ore bright and beautiful than the last—bright with the presence of that unseen Friend,

184

Who once on earth blessed little children—and beautiful with memories of a loving life, which has sought and found that truest kind of happiness, the only kind that is really worth the having, the happiness of making others happy too!

Your affectionate Friend,
Lewis Carroll
Christmas, 1871.

MY DEAR CHILD,

Please to fancy, if you can, that you are reading a real letter, from a real friend whom you have seen, and whose voice you can seem to yourself to hear, wishing you, as I do now with all my heart, a happy Easter.

Do you know that delicious dreamy feeling, when one first wakes on a summer morning, with the twitter of birds in the air, and the fresh breeze coming in at the open window— when, lying lazily with eyes half-shut, one sees as in a dream green boughs waving, or waters rippling in a golden light? It is a pleasure very near to sadness, bringing tears to one's eyes like a beautiful picture or poem. And is it not that a Mother's gentle hand that undraws your curtains, and a Mother's sweet voice that summons you to rise? To rise and forget, in the bright sunlight, the ugly dreams that frightened you so when all was dark—to rise and enjoy another happy day, first kneeling to thank that unseen Friend who sends you the beautiful sun?

Are these strange words from a writer of such tales as "Alice"? And is this a strange letter to find in a book of nonsense? It may be so. Some perhaps may blame me for thus mixing together things grave and gay; others may smile and think it odd that any one should speak of solemn things at all, except in Church and on a Sunday: but I think—nay, I am sure—that some children will read this gently and lovingly, and in the spirit in which I have written it.

For I do not believe God means us to thus to divide life into two halves—to wear a grave face on Sunday, and to think it out-of-place to even so much as mention Him on a week-day. Do you think He cares to see only kneeling figures and to hear only tones of prayer—and that He does not also love to see the lambs leaping in the sunlight, a and to hear the merry voices of the children, as they roll among the hay? Surely their innocent laughter is as sweet in His ears as the grandest anthem that ever rolled up from the "dim religious light" of some solemn cathedral?

And if I have written anything to add to those stores of innocent and healthy amusement that are laid up in books for the children I love so well, it is surely something I may hope to look back upon without shame and sorrow (as how much of life must then be recalled!) when my turn comes to walk through the valley of shadows.

This Easter sun will rise on you, dear child, feeling your "life in every limb," and eager to rush out into the fresh morning air—and many an Easter-day will come and go, before it finds you feeble and grey-headed, creeping wearily out to bask once more in the sunlight—but it is good, even now, to think sometimes of that great morning when the "Sun of Righteousness" shall "arise with healing in his wings."

Surely your gladness need not be the less for the thought that you will one day see a brighter dawn than this—when lovelier sights will meet your eyes than any waving trees or rippling waters—when angel-hands shall undraw your curtains, and sweeter tones than ever loving Mother breathed shall wake you to a new and glorious day—and when all the sadness, and the sin, that darkened life on this little earth, shall be forgotten like the dreams of a night that is past!

Your affectionate friend,
Lewis Carroll
Easter, 1876.

Sources

Alice's Adventures in Wonderland: The Evertype definitive edition,
by Lewis Carroll, 2016

Alice's Adventures in Wonderland, illus. June Lornie, 2013

Alice's Adventures in Wonderland, illus. Mathew Staunton, 2015

Alice's Adventures in Wonderland, illus. Harry Furniss, 2016

Alice's Adventures in Wonderland, illus. J. Michael Rolen, 2017

Through the Looking-Glass and What Alice Found There,
by Lewis Carroll, 2009

The Nursery "Alice", by Lewis Carroll, 2015

Alice's Adventures under Ground, by Lewis Carroll, 2009

The Hunting of the Snark, by Lewis Carroll, 2010

Sequels

A New Alice in the Old Wonderland, by Anna Matlack Richards, 2009

New Adventures of Alice, by John Rae, 2010

Alice Through the Needle's Eye, by Gilbert Adair, 2012

Wonderland Revisited and the Games Alice Played There,
by Keith Sheppard, 2009

Alice and the Boy who Slew the Jabberwock,
by Allan William Parkes, 2016

Spelling

Alice's Adventures in Wonderland,
Retold in words of one Syllable by Mrs J. C. Gorham, 2010

𐐈𐑊𐐮𐑅'𐑆 𐐈𐐼𐑂𐐯𐑌𐐽𐐲𐑉𐑆 𐐮𐑌 𐐎𐐲𐑌𐐼𐐲𐑉𐑊𐐰𐑌𐐼 (Alis'z Advenchurz in Wundurland), *Alice* printed in the Deseret Alphabet, 2014

𐐔 𐐘𐐭𐑌𐐻𐐮𐑍 𐐲𐑂 𐐔 𐐝𐑌𐐪𐑉𐐿 (Dh Hunting uv dh Snark),
The Hunting of the Snark printed in the Deseret Alphabet, 2016

𐐟𐑉𐐭 𐐔 𐐢𐐭𐐿𐐮𐑍-𐐘𐑊𐐰𐑅 𐐰𐑌𐐼 𐐘𐐶𐐲𐐻 𐐈𐑊𐐮𐑅 𐐙𐐱𐑌𐐼 𐐔𐐲𐑉
(Thru dh Lüking–Glas and Hwut Alis Fawnd Dher),
Looking-Glass printed in the Deseret Alphabet, 2016

Alice's Adventures in Wonderland,
Alice printed in Dyslexic-Friendly fonts, 2015

Through the Looking-Glass and What Alice Found There,
Looking-Glass printed in Dyslexic-Friendly fonts, 2020

ᗐᒪ∩ᔑ'ᔑ ᗋᗧ/ᘓ111 ᒍᖉᘓᔑ i11 ᗋ ᗞᐩᔑᒪ_ᘓᗧ∩ᔊ ᐯᎢ∩1ᗖᘓᖉ_ᗐ11ᗞ,
Alice printed in a font that simulates Dyslexia, 2015

𐑄𐑊 𐑄𐑉𐑂𐑄𐑉𐑌 𐑄𐑉𐑀𐑄𐑉𐑌 𐑄𐑉 𐑀𐑊𐑉𐑄𐑊𐑌 𐑄𐑉𐑌 (Ælisez
Ædvéntʃuɪz ɪn Wʌnduɪlænd), *Alice* printed in the Ewellic Alphabet, 2013

'Ælɪsɪz Əd'ventʃəz ɪn 'Wʌndə,lænd,
Alice printed in the International Phonetic Alphabet, 2014

Alis'z Advnĕrz in Wundland, *Alice* printed in the N̄spel orthography, 2015

ᔐᒪᒋᓭᒣᒍᔆ ᔐᔭᔑᒻᔐᓬᓴᒪᒻᒣ ᒪᔐ ᔑᓬᔐᒪᒻᔐᒪᔐᒻᔐᔕ,
Alice printed in the Nyctographic Square Alphabet, 2011

Alice's Adventures in Wonderland,
Alice printed in Pitman New Era Shorthand, forthcoming

Alice's Adventures in Wonderland, *Alice* printed in QR Codes, 2018

⸱ɔᴄɪƨ'ɿ ᴛᴛɪɪˈlꞁɔɿ ɪɪ ⸱ʃɪᴛˌᴐᴄɪˈɪ (Alɪs'əz ədventjuɪrz ɪn Wʌndərlænd),
Alice printed in the Shaw Alphabet, 2013

ALISIZ ADVENCꓶRZ IN WUNDⱤLAND,
Alice printed in the Unifon Alphabet, 2014

ᓂᐃXᗄ𐐎ᗄᓂᓄᔐ ᒋᒣᔐᒣᐈᔐᐯᗄᒻ ᐸᒣᗄᖘ (Aliz kalandjai Csodaországban),
The Hungarian *Alice* printed in Old Hungarian script, tr. Anikó Szilágyi, 2016

Elucidating Alice: A Textual Commentary on *Alice's Adventures in Wonderland*, by Selwyn Goodacre, 2015

Reflecting Alice: A Textual Commentary
on *Through the Looking-Glass*, by Selwyn Goodacre, 2021.

Behind the Looking-Glass: Reflections on the Myth
of Lewis Carroll, by Sherry L. Ackerman, 2012

Selections from the Lewis Carroll Collection
of Victoria J. Sewell, compiled by Byron W. Sewell, 2014

SOCIAL COMMENTARY

Clara in Blunderland, by Caroline Lewis, 2010

Lost in Blunderland: The further adventures of Clara,
by Caroline Lewis, 2010

John Bull's Adventures in the Fiscal Wonderland, by Charles Geake, 2010

The Westminster Alice, by H. H. Munro (Saki), 2017

Alice in Blunderland: An Iridescent Dream,
by John Kendrick Bangs, 2010

SIMULATIONS

Davy and the Goblin, by Charles Edward Carryl, 2010

The Admiral's Caravan, by Charles Edward Carryl, 2010

Gladys in Grammarland, by Audrey Mayhew Allen, 2010

Alice's Adventures in Pictureland, by Florence Adèle Evans, 2011

Folly in Fairyland, by Carolyn Wells, 2016

Rollo in Emblemland, by J. K. Bangs & C. R. Macauley, 2010

Phyllis in Piskie-land, by J. Henry Harris, 2012

Alice in Beeland, by Lillian Elizabeth Roy, 2012

Eileen's Adventures in Wordland, by Zillah K. Macdonald, 2010

Alice and the Time Machine, by Victor Fet, 2016

Алиса и Машина Времени (Alisa i Mashina Vremeni),
Alice and the Time Machine in Russian, tr. Victor Fet, 2016

SEWELLIANA

Sun-hee's Adventures Under the Land of Morning Calm,
by Victoria J. Sewell & Byron W. Sewell, 2016

선희의 조용한 아침의 나라 모험기 (Seonhuiui Joyonghan Achim-ui Nala
Moheomgi), *Sun-hee* in Korean, tr. Miyeong Kang, forthcoming

Alix's Adventures in Wonderland:
Lewis Carroll's Nightmare, by Byron W. Sewell, 2011

Áloþk's Adventures in Goatland, by Byron W. Sewell, 2011

Alice's Bad Hair Day in Wonderland, by Byron W. Sewell, 2012

The Carrollian Tales of Inspector Spectre, by Byron W. Sewell, 2011

The Annotated Alice in Nurseryland, by Byron W. Sewell, 2016

The Haunting of the Snarkasbord, by Alison Tannenbaum,
Byron W. Sewell, Charlie Lovett, & August A. Imholtz, Jr, 2012

Snarkmaster, by Byron W. Sewell, 2012

In the Boojum Forest, by Byron W. Sewell, 2014

Murder by Boojum, by Byron W. Sewell, 2014

Close Encounters of the Snarkian Kind, by Byron W. Sewell, 2016

TRANSLATIONS

Кайкалдыҥ Јеринде Алисала болгон учуралдар (Kaykaldıñ Cerinde
Alisala bolgon uçuraldar), *Alice* in Altai, tr. Küler Tepukov, 2016

Alice's Adventures in An Appalachian Wonderland,
Alice in Appalachian English, tr. Byron & Victoria Sewell, 2012

Սնարքի Որսը (Snarki Orsě),
The Hunting of the Snark in Eastern Armenian,
tr. Alexander Kalantaryan & Artak Kalantaryan, forthcoming

Ալիս Հրաշալիքներու Աշխարհին Մէջ (Alis Hrashalikneru Ashkharhin Mēch),
Alice in Western Armenian, tr. Yervant Gobelean, forthcoming

Patimatli ali Alice tu Vāsilia ti Ciudii,
Alice in Aromanian, tr. Mariana Bara, 2015

Элисәнең Сәйерстандағы мажаралары (Älisäneñ Säyerstandağı majaraları), *Alice* in Bashkir, tr. Güzäl Sitdykova, 2017

Алесіны прыгоды ў Цудаземʼі (Alesiny pryhody u Tsudazemʼi), *Alice* in Belarusian, tr. Max Ščur, 2016

На тым баку Люстра і што там напаткала Алесю (Na tym baku Liustra i shto tam napatkala Alesiu), *Looking-Glass* in Belarusian, tr. Max Ščur, 2016

Снаркаловы (Snarkalovy), *The Hunting of the Snark* in Belarusian, tr. Max Ščur, forthcoming

Troioù-kaer Alis e Vro ar Marzhoù, *Alice* in Breton, tr. Herve Kerrain, forthcoming

Crystal's Adventures in A Cockney Wonderland, *Alice* in Cockney Rhyming Slang, tr. Charlie Lovett, 2015

Aventurs Alys in Pow an Anethow, *Alice* in Cornish, tr. Nicholas Williams, 2015

Aventurs Alys in Pow an Anethow Dyllans Dywyêthek Kernowek-Sowsnek, *Alice* in Cornish, bilingual edition, tr. Nicholas Williams, 2021

Alice's Ventures in Wunderland, *Alice* in Cornu-English, tr. Alan M. Kent, 2015

Maries Hændelser i Vidunderlandet, *Alice* in Danish, tr. D.G., forthcoming

آلیس در سرزمین عجایب (Âlis dar Sarzamin-e Ajâyeb), *Alice* in Dari, tr. Rahman Arman, 2015

Äventyrä Alice i Underlandä, *Alice* in Elfdalian, tr. Inga-Britt Petersson, forthcoming

La Aventuroj de Alicio en Mirlando, *Alice* in Esperanto, tr. E. L. Kearney (1910), 2009

La Aventuroj de Alico en Mirlando, *Alice* in Esperanto, tr. Donald Broadribb, 2012

Trans la Spegulo kaj kion Alico trovis tie, *Looking-Glass* in Esperanto, tr. Donald Broadribb, 2012

Les Aventures d'Alice au pays des merveilles, *Alice* in French, tr. Henri Bué, 2015

Les Aventures d'Alice au pays des merveilles,
Alice in French, tr. Henri Bué, illus. Mathew Staunton, 2015

ელისის თავგადასავალი საოცრებათა ქვეყანაში (Elisis t'avgadasavali
saoc'rebat a k'veqanaši), *Alice* in Georgian, tr. Giorgi Gokieli, 2016

Alice's Abenteuer im Wunderland,
Alice in German, tr. Antonie Zimmermann, 2010

Die Lissel ehr Erlebnisse im Wunnerland,
Alice in Palantine German, tr. Franz Schlosser, 2013

Der Alice ihre Obmteier im Wunderlaund,
Alice in Viennese German, tr. Hans Werner Sokop, 2012

Balþos Gadedeis Aþalhaidais in Sildaleikalanda,
Alice in Gothic, tr. David Alexander Carlton, 2015

Nā Hana Kupanaha a ʻĀleka ma ka ʻĀina Kamahaʻo,
Alice in Hawaiian, tr. R. Keao NeSmith, 2017

Nā Hana Kupanaha a ʻĀleka ma ka ʻĀina Kamahaʻo
Kope ʻōlelo Hawaiʻi-ʻōlelo Pelekānia,
Alice in Hawaiian, bilingual edition, tr. R. Keao NeSmith, 2022

Ma Loko o ke Aniani Kū a me ka Mea i Loaʻa iā ʻĀleka
ma Laila, *Looking-Glass* in Hawaiian, tr. R. Keao NeSmith, 2017

Aliz kalandjai Csodaországban,
Alice in Hungarian, tr. Anikó Szilágyi, 2013

Ævintýri Lísu í Undralandi, *Alice* in Icelandic, tr. Þórarinn Eldjárn, 2013

L'Aventuri di Alicia en Marvelia, *Alice* in Ido, tr. Gonçalo Neves, 2020

Le Aventuras de Alice in le Pais del Meravilias,
Alice in Interlingua, tr. Rodrigo Guerra, 2020

Eachtra Eibhlíse i dTír na nIontas,
Alice in Irish, tr. Pádraig Ó Cadhla (1922), 2015

Eachtraí Eilíse i dTír na nIontas, *Alice* in Irish, tr. Nicholas Williams, 2007

Eachtraí Eilíse i dTír na nIontas: Eagrán Dátheangach Gaeilge-Béarla,
Alice in Irish, bilingual edition, tr. tr. Nicholas Williams, 2022

Lastall den Scáthán agus a bhFuair Eilís Ann Roimpi,
Looking-Glass in Irish, tr. Nicholas Williams, 2009

Le Avventure di Alice nel Paese delle Meraviglie,
Alice in Italian, tr. Teodorico Pietrocòla Rossetti, 2010

Alis Advencha ina Wandalan,
Alice in Jamaican Creole, tr. Tamirand Nnena De Lisser, 2016

L's Aventuthes d'Alice en Êmèrvil'lie,
Alice in Jèrriais, tr. Geraint Williams, 2012

L'Travèrs du Mitheux et chein qu'Alice y dêmuchit,
Looking-Glass in Jèrriais, tr. Geraint Williams, 2012

Алисэ Тэлъыджэщӏым зэрыщылар (Alisė Tel′ydzhėshchḣym
zėryshchyḣar), *Alice* in Kabardian, tr. Murat Temyr & Murat Brat, 2020

Алиса Къужур Дунияны Къыдырады (Alisa Qujur Duniyanı
Qıdıradı), *Alice* in Karachay-Balkar, tr. Magomet Gekki, 2019

Әлисәнің ғажайып елдегі басынан кешкендері (Älïsäniñ ğajayıp
eldegi basınan keşkenderi), *Alice* in Kazakh, tr. Fatima Moldashova, 2016

Алисаның Хайхастар Чирінзер чорығы (Alīsanıñ Hayhastar Çīrinzer
çorığı), *Alice* in Khakas, tr. Maria Çertykova, 2017

Алисакӧд Шемӧсмуын лоӧмторъяс (Alisaköd Šemösmuyn loömtor″ias),
Alice in Komi-Zyrian, tr. Evgenii Tsypanov & Elena Eltsova, 2018

Алисанын Кызыктар Өлкөсүндөгү укмуштуу окуялары
(Alisanın Kızıktar Ölkösündögü ukmuştuu okuyaları),
Alice in Kyrgyz, tr. Aida Egemberdieva, 2016

Las Aventuras de Alisia en el Paiz de las Maraviyas,
Alice in Ladino, tr. Avner Perez, 2016

לאס אב'ינטוראס די אליסייה אין איל פאאיס די לאס מאראב'יליייאס
(Las Aventuras de Alisia en el Paiz de las Maraviyas),
Alice in Ladino, tr. Avner Perez, 2016

Alisis pīdzeivuojumi Breinumu zemē,
Alice in Latgalian, tr. Evika Muizniece, 2015

Alicia in Terrā Mīrābilī, *Alice* in Latin, tr. Clive Harcourt Carruthers, 2018

Alicia in Terrā Mīrābilī: Ēditiō Bilinguis Latīna et Anglica,
Alice in Latin, bilingual edition, tr. Clive Harcourt Carruthers, 2021

Aliciae per Speculum Trānsitus (Quaeque Ibi Invēnit),
Looking-Glass in Latin, tr. Clive Harcourt Carruthers, forthcoming

Alisa-ney Aventuras in Divalanda, *Alice* in Lingua de Planeta (Lidepla),
tr. Anastasia Lysenko & Dmitry Ivanov, 2014

La aventuras de Alisia en la país de mervelias,
Alice in Lingua Franca Nova, tr. Simon Davies, 2012

Alice ehr Eventüürn in't Wunnerland,
Alice in Low German, tr. Reinhard F. Hahn, 2010

Contoyrtyssyn Ealish ayns Çheer ny Yindyssyn,
Alice in Manx, tr. Brian Stowell, 2010

Ko Ngā Takahanga i a Ārihi i Te Ao Mīharo,
Alice in Māori, tr. Tom Roa, 2015

Dee Erläwnisse von Alice em Wundalaund,
Alice in Mennonite Low German, tr. Jack Thiessen, 2012

Auanturiou adelis en Bro an Marthou,
Alice in Middle Breton, tr. Herve Le Bihan & Herve Kerrain, forthcoming

The Aventures of Alys in Wondyr Lond,
Alice in Middle English, tr. Brian S. Lee, 2013

Þurh þe Loking-Glas and What Alys Founde Þere,
Looking-Glass in Middle English, tr. Brian S. Lee, forthcoming

L'Avventure d'Alice 'int' 'o Paese d' 'e Maraveglie,
Alice in Neapolitan, tr. Roberto D'Ajello, 2016

Attravierzo 'o specchio e cchello c'Alice ce truvaie,
Looking-Glass in Neapolitan, tr. Roberto D'Ajello, 2019

L'Aventuros de Alis in Marvoland, *Alice* in Neo, tr. Ralph Midgley, 2013

Elises Eventyr i Undernes Land: den første norske *Alice:*
Elise's Adventures in the Land of Wonders: the first Norwegian *Alice,*
Alice in Norwegian, ed. & tr. Anne Kristin Lande, 2022

Alice sine opplevingar i Eventyrlandet,
Alice in Nynorsk, tr. Sigrun Anny Røssbø, 2020

Æðelgyðe Ellendæda on Wundorlande,
Alice in Old English, tr. Peter S. Baker, 2015

La geste d'Aalis el Païs de Merveilles,
Alice in Old French, tr. May Plouzeau, 2017

Alice's Adventchers in Wunderland,
Alice in Scouse, tr. Marvin R. Sumner, 2015

Mbalango wa Alice eTikweni ra Swihlamariso,
Alice in Shangani, tr. Peniah Mabaso & Steyn Khesani Madlome, 2015

Ahlice's Aveenturs in Wunderlaant,
Alice in Border Scots, tr. Cameron Halfpenny, 2015

Alice's Mishanters in e Land o Farlies,
Alice in Caithness Scots, tr. Catherine Byrne, 2014

Alice's Adventirs in Wunnerlaun,
Alice in Glaswegian Scots, tr. Thomas Clark, 2014

Ailice's Anters in Ferlielann,
Alice in North-East Scots (Doric), tr. Derrick McClure, 2012

Throwe the Keekin-Gless an Fit Ailice's Funn There,
Looking-Glass in North-East Scots (Doric), tr. Derrick McClure, 2021

Alice's Adventirs in Wonderlaand,
Alice in Shetland Scots, tr. Laureen Johnson, 2012

Ailice's Aventurs in Wunnerland,
Alice in Southeast Central Scots, tr. Sandy Fleemin, 2011

Ailis's Anterins i the Laun o Ferlies,
Alice in Synthetic Scots, tr. Andrew McCallum, 2013

Alice's Carrànts in Wunnerlan,
Alice in Ulster Scots, tr. Anne Morrison-Smyth, 2013

Alison's Jants in Ferlieland,
Alice in West-Central Scots, tr. James Andrew Begg, 2014

Alice muNyika yeMashiripiti,
Alice in Shona, tr. Shumirai Nyota & Tsitsi Nyoni, 2015

Алисаның қайғаллығ Черинде полған чоруқтары (Alisaniñ qayğallığ
Çerinde polğan çoruqtarı), *Alice* in Shor, tr. Liubov' Arbaçakova, 2017

Alicia's Adventuras en Wonderlandia,
Alice in Spanglish, tr. Ilan Stavans, 2021

Alis bu Cëlmo dac Cojube w dat Tantelat,
Alice in Ṣurayt, tr. Jan Bet-Ṣawoce, 2015

Alisi Ndani ya Nchi ya Ajabu, *Alice* in Swahili, tr. Ida Hadjuvayanis, 2015

Alices Äventyr i Sagolandet, *Alice* in Swedish, tr. Emily Nonnen, 2010

'Alisi 'i he Fonua 'o e Fakaofo',
Alice in Tongan, tr. Siutāula Cocker & Telesia Kalavite, 2014

De Aventure Alisu in Mirviziländ,
Alice in Uropi, tr. Bertrand Carette & Joël Landais, 2018

Ventürs jiela Lälid in Stunalän, *Alice* in Volapük,
tr. Ralph Midgley, forthcoming

Lès-avirètes da Alice ô payis dès mèrvèyes,
Alice in Walloon, tr. Jean-Luc Fauconnier, 2012

Lès paskéyes d'Alice è payis dès mèrvèyes,
Alice in Central Walloon, tr. Bernard Louis, 2017

Anturiaethau Alys yng Ngwlad Hud, *Alice* in Welsh, tr. Selyf Roberts, 2010

I Avventur de Alìs ind el Paes di Meravìli,
Alice in Western Lombard, tr. GianPietro Gallinelli, 2015

U-Alisi Kwilizwe Lemimangaliso,
Alice in Xhosa, tr. Mhlobo Jadezweni, forthcoming

Di Avantures fun Alis in Vunderland,
Alice in Yiddish, tr. Joan Braman, 2015

Alises Avantures in Vunderland, *Alice* in Yiddish, tr. Adina Bar-El, 2018

אַליסעס אַוואַנטורעס אין וונדערלאַנד (Alises Avantures in Vunderland),
Alice in Yiddish, tr. Adina Bar-El, 2018

Insumansumane Zika-Alice,
Alice in Zimbabwean Ndebele, tr. Dion Nkomo, 2015

U-Alice Ezweni Lezimanga, *Alice* in Zulu, tr. Bhekinkosi Ntuli, 2014

www.ingramcontent.com/pod-product-compliance
Lightning Source LLC
Chambersburg PA
CBHW020319260626
47156CB00004B/1289